# THE GLITTERING EYE

*Also by L.J. Adlington*

The Diary of Pelly D
Cherry Heaven

*Other titles from Hodder Children's Books*

Jackdaw Summer
Clay
The Fire-Eaters
Skellig
Heaven Eyes
Kit's Wilderness
Secret Heart
Counting Stars
*David Almond*

Red Moon
Pizza on Saturday
The Flight of the Emu
MOVING TIMES SEQUENCE:
Bloom of Youth
Grandmother's Footsteps
Stronger than Mountains
*Rachel Anderson*

# THE
# GLITTERING
# EYE

## L.J.
## ADLINGTON

Hodder
Children's
Books

a division of Hachette Children's Books

First published in Great Britain in 2009
by Hodder Children's Books

Quotes from *The Discovery of the Tomb of Tutankhamen* by Howard Carter
and A. C. Mace reprinted with kind permission from Dover Publications Inc.

Quotes from *A Thousand Miles Up the Nile* by Amelia B. Edwards
reprinted with kind permission from Trotamundas Press Ltd.

1

A Catalogue record for this book is available from the British Library

ISBN-13: 978 0 340 95681 6

Typeset in Berkeley Book by Avon DataSet Ltd,
Bidford on Avon, Warwickshire

Printed and bound in Great Britain by
CPI Bookmarque Ltd, Croydon, Surrey

The paper and board used in this paperback by Hodder Children's Books
are natural recyclable products made from wood grown in
sustainable forests. The manufacturing processes conform to the
environmental regulations of the country of origin.

Hodder Children's Books
a division of Hachette Children's Books
338 Euston Road, London NW1 3BH
An Hachette UK company
www.hachette.co.uk

For Margaret Lilian Tyers
1921–2007

*also*

Mr C. W. Cluskey, Village Headmaster
1924–1994

# 1 In the Barley Field

*May you go forth by day,*
*May you join the sun disc*
*And may his rays illuminate your face*
                              *(Book of the Dead)*

He woke up in a barley field.

For a while he just lay there, flat on his back, with his arms outstretched and his right hand curled in a fist. Something soft and furry tickled his cheek. He opened his mouth to swallow down warm air, like someone dying of thirst gulping a cool drink of water.

His eyes were dry and crusted – had he been asleep for a while? He squinted up at a fuzz of green and gold waving against a naked blue sky. Words came into his head.

*Barley . . . Tickly . . .*

*Sun . . . Hot . . .*

1

*Ground . . . Hard.*

Pain crinkled his legs as he moved them. The soles of his feet were a raw pinky-brown and clean, as if he'd never taken a step in his life – which, for all he knew, he never had. He hoisted himself upright, swaying like the barley. As he took his first steps the dry soil was scuffed up into scabby patches, revealing a damp, dark brown underneath.

*Good for growing things in*, he thought, then, *How did I know that?*

When he put out his hands to steady himself he found he was carrying a piece of . . . *wood*, yes, *wood*, that's what it was called. Two pieces of wood braced at an angle and ending with a dull metal blade. He had no idea what it was for, nor the scratchy thing strapped to his shoulder, for that matter.

Before he could properly balance himself, the ground began to shudder. He turned round and round quickly, looking for something called *danger*. The ground rippled so violently he was afraid he'd be shaken right off it. Suddenly, startlingly, a large white hippopotamus came crashing right through the middle of the field, running straight towards him. Its mouth was open, showing giant teeth and a fat, pink tongue. Four hefty feet trampled the barley and the soil.

He yelped – the first sound he had heard himself make. He jumped to one side. The hippo never flinched. It stomped past, quickly followed by a new noise. What sort of sound was it? A gruffling? Grouching? Grallaking? No. *Growling*, that was the word. Growling and barking. Dogs!

For one moment he had a picture in his mind of speedy lean creatures running alongside him, with tongues hanging out and eyes bright with excitement. Yes, he knew dogs, but he'd never seen ones like these two before, all squat bodies and savage tempers. Their faces had a jackal-look about them and their barks held the promise of pain. He didn't wait to find out how sharp the yellowed teeth were. He turned and ran down the wide trail left by the speeding hippo, his bare feet ripped open on the crumpled barley stalks. He was quickly learning that whoever he was, wherever he was, he wanted to be safe.

Without warning he broke out of the field. Having only air to fight against he pitched forward and stumbled a few steps across dark, damp ground. Thick clumps of grass and reeds sprouted up before him, following the line of something wide and wet straight ahead.

A river!

An old remembered cunning told him dogs couldn't

track across water, even if they could swim. All he had to do was plunge right in and hide among the reeds until the vicious beasts grew bored. Once they gave up the chase he could slink across the river to the other side.

He skidded down a muddy ridge and floundered as quietly as possible into the brown water. It was wonderfully cool on his skin, though the cuts on his feet sizzled with pain. He half waded, half swam towards a green sward of marsh plants spreading into the river where the current was slack. He went more carefully when he caught glimpses of creatures – *birds*, were they called? – moving through the sedge. He didn't want to disturb anything that might give his hiding place away. Once settled and safe the sounds of the river tickled his ears: water rippled, long stems rustled, hoarse voices croaked in secret places. Over on the bank the dogs ran wild, barking in their own coarse language. Let them bark!

Something new caught his attention – a tawny slinking thing with golden eyes and long whiskers. For a moment he relived the sensation of fur brushing his cheek. It was a cat. He suddenly knew it, as surely as he knew that cats hunted birds.

*No, no, no, not here, Cat. Go look for your dinner somewhere I'm not!*

The cat kept creeping across the matted plants until the very thing he dreaded happened: one bird called warning, causing a flock of lapwings and tiny sparrows to shoot up from the marsh, calling *danger! danger! danger!*

A host of other birds answered the cry, making a storm of feathers in the air, too many for him to see or name. There was no time for him to wish for wings of his own. He pushed out from the greenery and began to thrash in the open water, somehow keeping hold of his wooden tool and basket all the while. He had no idea that one clump of reeds hid a gnarled brown beast, savouring the sight of a helpless human. This impossibly fat crocodile submerged silently and followed the taste of blood trickling from his feet. It wouldn't attack as long as the cat patrolled the riverbank. After that . . .

Up on dry land the cat licked grass seeds from its fur and watched the boy draw closer to the far side of the river, where reeds soon gave way to a great plain of red sand that shimmered in the heat. Beyond that, mountains glared red and gold in the sun. Arching over their jagged summits was endless blue sky, entirely bare of clouds.

Then came a new sound, not a dog's bark or a bird's cry. A man walked out of the barley to the river, with the sun blazing behind him. One word cracked the air.

*'Stop!'*

The boy's arms suddenly flopped to his side, and his legs went limp too. He sank down then bobbed up again, spitting some water out of his mouth, choking on the rest. His toes found the shallow river bottom, just keeping his eyes and nose above water. He was half aware of a new fear – that submerged snakes would come coiling round his legs.

'Rip! Bite! Over here, now!'

The dogs bounded towards the man giving high-pitched yips of pent-up violence.

'Stay!'

Like the boy they were obedient, dropping to their bellies at the order. There was fear and love in their eyes as they watched the man walk to the river edge.

He was tall – almost as tall as the barley – with dark and dusty skin. Hair sprouted from his scalp in black plaits, like clumps of angry spiders. His arms, shoulders and legs were thick with . . . the boy struggled for the word, *muscles*. No, more than that. *Power*. What was the man carrying? Certainly not a soggy basket. The boy flexed his own fingers as if he remembered carrying something like it himself, before he woke up with his strange stick of wood. Yes, he knew what the man wielded, even though he hadn't quite remembered what it could do.

It was a whip.

In his mind he heard its sharp song.

The man casually uncoiled the whip. 'Running back to the red lands, are you? What sort of beast have I caught? No claws, no sting, no fangs spitting poison . . . Ha! Look at that fierce face, Rip! It's a runt. A stunted little manling that thinks it can fight us! You could swallow him down in two mouthfuls and still have room for more, couldn't you, you nasty mongrel? Well, that changes things a bit. Come back to the bank, *shabti*, that's right, over here. In front of me. Stand up straight! Look smart when I'm talking to you. Yes, keep your eyes on my whip. Know what it's for? Makes you shake, doesn't it? That's nothing to how it will make you scream if I catch you running away again!'

Immediately the boy swam back to the shore. *Shabti*, the man had called him, so Shabti became his name.

He discovered what sweat was when large drops of it rolled down his forehead and into his eyes, mixing with trickles of river water. He was desperate to get away from the whip and the dogs, but the man's words had a strange hold over him. He dragged all his willpower to a hard ball inside and looked straight into the man's furrowed scowl, defying it.

No use.

As soon as the man said, 'Step forward,' he did just that. His world exploded as a fist punched into his face.

The man rubbed his knuckles and grinned, while the dogs barked their excitement. 'When I talk to you, keep your eyes fixed on the floor, get it?'

'Yes.'

Amazingly, this word came out of his own blood-tasting mouth.

'Yes, what?'

'Er . . . yes what.'

'No, you thick-witted fool! Say, *Yes, Master.*'

Instinctively Shabti tried to swallow the words down. He couldn't.

'Yes, Master.'

A cunning gleam lit the man's eyes. 'Say, *Yes, Master Hob.* No, no, wait, say, *Yes, Master Hob, I am nothing but stinking dung.*'

'Yes, Master Hob, I am . . . nothing but . . . stinking dung.'

What was dung? What was stinking? What was *I* for that matter? No chance to ask. Master Hob had him by the arm and was twisting him round to look over the river.

'A word of advice, boy. If I were you, I'd think very carefully about going near the river again. You were lucky Lady Hippo didn't squash you in one of her

8

tantrums, or that that treacherous crocodile there didn't bite you in two, pull you down and wedge you on the riverbed till your flesh was nice and rotten – tender enough to be torn from your bones without any trouble. And that's not all, 'cause you see, no matter how quick the crocodiles are, they're helpless as kittens when the *real* predators come from the red lands. Those *Deshret* monsters take great pleasure skinning crocs while they're still alive . . .'

Hob enjoyed seeing Shabti go white with fear. Then his tone changed, though the nasty glitter in his eyes didn't diminish.

'Off you go now,' he said lightly. 'Back into the barley with you.'

'I can go?'

'Yes – hop it. Don't worry, the dogs'll stay with me.'

In a heartbeat he was away from the river and plunging through the barley. Hob had let him go! He was free after all! The field was so vast he could soon become lost again, try another way of escaping. He'd be clever this time. They'd never know where he was hiding, never . . .

'*Shabti!* Where are you?'

Immediately Shabti's whole body convulsed and he stopped dead. Even though he put his free hand over his

9

mouth and bit down hard he couldn't stop the words vomiting out.

'Here I am!' he answered once, then a second time, 'Here I am!'

Master Hob sauntered up, jeering *ha ha ha*. 'Now do you understand, Shabti? *You can't run away.* Whenever I call, you have to answer me. You have to do whatever I say. Understand?'

'Yes ... I mean, yes, Master Hob.'

'Good. Now follow me. You've work to do. Endless, backbreaking work!'

Work it was then.

Whatever that meant.

'Before you start I'll teach you a favourite saying of mine – *A boy's ears are in his back. He doesn't hear until you beat him*.'

With these words Hob brandished his whip.

Every lash brought a shout of pain and outrage from the boy. Over and over his mind protested – *What have I done to deserve this?*

# 2 Going Underground

*The place is ghostly and peopled by nightmares.*
(Amelia B. Edwards, *A Thousand Miles Up the Nile*)

Too much sky – too much light!

Amy Clayton crammed her sunglasses on and kept her gaze low. December in Egypt was nothing like England's grey rain. Here there were no clouds and the sun was like a great glaring eye.

She was stuck between arriving and knowing what to do next.

Clusters of men glanced at her from the kiosks and corners of the concrete strip outside Luxor Airport. Not threatening. Curious. Entertained, even, by the strange sight she presented in the dusty heat – her black and red plaits, black boots, ripped black jeans. The men squinted at the glitter of her aggressive jewellery, and the raincoat stuffed in a strap of her backpack. Not far off an army of bony brown cats scavenged round a rubbish bin. They scattered as a nearby car engine choked to life.

Sun, men, cats – Amy ignored all of them.

No sign of her dad anywhere. What to do next?

A hand tugged at her backpack.

'Hey! Get off that!'

She wrestled it away from a tall, straw-haired boy about her own age, dressed in dusty jeans and a crisp white shirt – sleeves rolled up to display a tan.

'Just trying to help you to a taxi,' the boy said. 'You're Amy Clayton, right?'

'I can carry my own bag! Where's my dad?'

'Busy at the dig, so he sent me to meet you. I'm Jason Henderson . . .'

'I know who you are, and yes, I have seen you on telly with Dad. Last time we met for real you picked your nose and ate your own snot.'

His famous as-seen-on-TV smile vanished. 'That was five years ago! And I didn't, anyway.'

'Did.'

'Let's just go, shall we?'

Amy wouldn't get in the taxi at first – there was no seat belt.

Jason said fine, she could walk to the desert.

'The driver's smoking!' she hissed, once in the car.

'Welcome to Egypt,' was the only reply.

'Egypt *stinks*,' Charlotte Pratt had informed everyone at school. Charlotte's experience of Egypt was based on a quick trip to Cairo at the height of summer during a power cut. 'The pyramids are *way* small and the whole city smells of blocked sewers and they *burn* dirty toilet paper instead of flushing it, and the pollution's, like, really bad, and there are dead horses just lying in the streets. You'll love it, Amy. You'll fit right in.'

Jason began an enthusiastic explanation of the sights they passed.

Amy filtered his voice out, thinking, *Save it for the cameras, wonder boy.*

The taxi dodged donkey carts and battered vans. Billboards, apartment blocks, mosques and markets – the town of Luxor spread its sun-coloured stones along the banks of the river. Amy stared at ancient monuments from behind the secrecy of her sunglasses. Columns, towers and great gateways . . . everything was god-sized. She felt very small.

They nosed through a jam of geriatric cars to a long promenade, and there it was . . . The legendary River Nile. Beyond that, the desert.

13

The sky was so wide over there! It spread out for ever, too vast to be blue, too dry for clouds. The desert cliffs were dense lumps of red squatting on the horizon.

'The west bank,' Jason said. 'Once known as Thebes. That's where the ancient dead are buried – set to rest in their rocky tombs for all eternity.'

As presenter of the hit TV show *Action Archaeology!* Amy's dad was being paid to dig them up.


'Why would I want to spend Christmas in Egypt?' Amy had moaned when the idea was first mooted.

'Well you can't stay here,' Mum said at once. 'Not with the builders still plastering the nursery, and Claire'll need your bedroom till the baby comes.'

'Cheers, Claire, for making me homeless.'

'Don't talk to your sister like that!'

'Fine, take her side again!'

Claire said, 'Seriously, Ames, you've always wanted to go to Egypt. Remember when you used to fancy Tutankhamun? You'll be back in time for the birth and baby-sitting duties. Don't tell me you'd rather go stay with Grandma Clayton and her nasty doggies?'

Amy began, 'I'd rather . . .' then stopped. Rather what? Rather have everyone at least pretend she wasn't some sort of distasteful stain they couldn't scrub clean? Rather turn back time to when she didn't feel she had to skulk in corners or apologize for her very existence? Rather not feel like guilt incarnate every time someone glanced in her direction?

Dad's only contribution to the debate was a flustered, 'Doesn't anybody realize the pressure I'm under for this new series?'

They motored across the Nile in a noisy boat. Jumping on board made Amy wince. Pills never quite killed the pain of her cracked ribs. There was no forgetting her injuries, no matter how whole she looked on the outside. She flinched again when Jason put out a hand to help her out of the boat.

The road on the far side quickly took them away from the river's cooling breezes and into the dry landscape of the desert edge. Scrubby plants struggled for life as long as possible before rocks ruled completely. The cliffs weren't high enough to block the sun, nothing could, but they were still overwhelming and somehow grotesque, as if they'd been created from a deformed mould. Where the rock was exposed to light it glowed a warm, pale orange. At the foot of the cliffs cascades of white stones mixed with drab sand. There were valleys eroded in the high plateau, each reaching into the rocks like a spidery hand with knobbly knuckles.

'Which valley are you filming in?'

'You don't say *valley*,' Jason corrected her. 'It's *wadi*.'

'Fine. Which wadi?'

'The Windy Wadi.'

Their bus dropped them at the beginning of a featureless path between the cliffs. As they walked along it, the real world fell away and they were quickly surrounded by the desert plateau. It made no effort to impress. It simply *was*. Sun, rocks, sky. Nothing else, unless you could count the uncomfortable sense of *immanence* – as if some ageless spirit lived in the elements, just on the edge of understanding.

The path fanned out and they arrived. Their only welcome was a wave from a tall man in a turban who stood at a spoil heap of debris, watching over a convoy of dusty workers dragging old tyres full of further rocks to add to the pile. Jason said he was the Egyptian overseer – Farouk.

Amy looked around the wadi. So this was where the *Action Archaeology!* team would conjure up marvels for their primetime slot on the Discovery Channel. What was all the fuss about? She'd imagined a super-slick operation in a glamorous setting, with private trailers for the presenters and top-notch technology. This place all looked very home-made and uncomfortable.

Pathways were marked with string tied round sticks jammed in the ground. Wooden chicken baskets were stacked like primitive skyscrapers. One faded green awning provided shade for a couple of rickety plastic chairs. There was no breeze. No noise either, save for the sound of rocks sliding and men murmuring. Amy struggled to breathe the heavy air.

'Why's it called Windy Wadi?'

Jason smirked. 'Because it's not.'

'Ha ha.' She looked around but saw only Egyptian men in their long galabeya tunics. 'Where's my dad?'

'Probably trying to be in two places at once.'

That sounded about right.

She spotted a dark hole high on a steep slope of stones to her right, on the north side of the wadi. There it was, the cause of all the upheaval. The one bit of darkness in all the aching light.

'Ready to go underground?' Jason asked.

No! That was absolutely the last thing she felt like doing. Looking at the tomb entrance there on the slope, Amy couldn't help shrivelling inside.

Why did people have to dig up things that were best left buried?

# 3 Kemet

*My bread is of white wheat, my beer is of red barley . . .*
*(Book of the Dead)*

There was no shelter, no escape. A tight web of pain gripped the back of his skull, matched only by a grinding ache deep in his left hip.

*Shabti!*

The name clanged and echoed in his head long after Master Hob had finished bellowing at him. Hob was rarely out of sight and never beyond hearing. The two dogs, Rip and Bite, dodged around the fields, sometimes chasing mice, sometimes trouble.

How long had he been working already? No idea. First there'd been a field of beans, going down row after row of plants so healthy they almost glowed green. Unfortunately the weeds were bursting with life too.

When he looked back along a row he'd just cleared he could already see cheeky little shoots bursting through the dark soil behind him.

Weeding was done using the strange wooden tool he held in his right hand. *Hoe*, it was called. He had to stoop to wield it with enough force to break through the ground, then toss the weed over his shoulder to the crumpled reed basket on his back. He obviously wasn't used to holding a hoe. The smooth wood gave him raging red blisters so fat it was agony just to grip the handle. Whenever he tried to straighten up, Hob's whip snapped through the air and his voice growled, 'Work!' So work he did.

His mind kept as busy as his body. Even the hot sun couldn't burn all the questions out of his head. He heard the constant buzz of a wasp in his ear but although he swiped at the air with increasing frustration, he never saw it, let alone swatted it away. He kept alert for more serious danger. Where was the white hippo? Was it wallowing in the cool waters of the river? Was it afraid of the dangers from Deshret? Hardly. What could possibly threaten a full-grown hippo?

A quick flash of memory startled him and he thought he had a spear in his hand. The moment passed. He held a hoe again.

Once the beans were hoed, work began on miles of ripening peas. Hours passed – or was it longer? The sun stubbornly stayed high in the sky, refusing to rush day into night. There were other brown figures in the fields, all adults – no children. Some weeded, some harvested. 'Don't we get to eat soon?' he asked them in a low voice.

Their astonished expressions were all the answer he got. Apparently the workers were *not* supposed to eat anything. Only, when would they drink? He'd barely managed a few mouthfuls of the brackish river water; now he didn't have enough saliva in his mouth to swallow, and licking the salty sweat off his top lip only made his thirst worse. He wondered if there'd be a chance to scuttle over to one of the water channels dug between the fields to irrigate crops. That could wait. For now he was desperate to eat, whatever the risk of Hob's anger. Pea pods were ripening almost before his very eyes. Surely it wasn't a crime to try just one . . . ? He snapped a pod – the sound seemed to echo around the field – and used one dirty nail to prise it open, nipping each perfect little pea from the soft pod lining. Oh, they were so sweet! The best food he'd ever tasted! Maybe they'd rattle around his hollow stomach, but now he had hope he wouldn't starve.

Yes, hope.

Hope that the work would soon be over. Hope that he'd find a way to escape that didn't involve dodging crocodiles on the way to Deshret. If only Hob didn't spot him and make him answer with such agonizing obedience – *Here I am!*

Work again.

He became so wrapped up in his own aches and aggravations, it took a while for him to notice that the pea plants were beginning to shrivel, drying out and withering before his very eyes. Even the weeds seemed to lose heart. They slumped to the ground and were limp when he loosened them from the soil. The sun eventually dipped so low the wooden sticks supporting the peas cast spear-shaped shadows across the ground. Only then could he see beyond the fields to a beautiful white house surrounded by shady trees and a high wall.

He smiled with cracked lips. Now *that* was the sort of house he wanted to go home to!

As if in answer to his thoughts, a deep bell note signalled the end of the working day. Time for the servants to straighten up, steady their baskets and march away. Quick – Shabti grabbed his own basket and dropped into line, looking nothing like as tall and serene as the others. They moved in silence, making stark black silhouettes against the newly-red sky. Soon they reached a low mud wall at the edge of the fields. It marked the border of a busy compound, crammed with workshops and storerooms. Workers arrived from every part of the estate. It was amazing to see how many crops had been gathered. A stocky overseer called Reniseb tallied the full baskets and signalled each worker to take their food to the appropriate store.

Shabti stepped up to the gate. Reniseb's lip curled when she saw the proffered basket of weeds.

'You snivelling little beast! Empty this on the compost heap and go straight to the Night House!'

What was a compost heap? Shabti didn't dare ask. He stumbled out of line before being trampled in the rhythm of marching feet.

The compound was an extraordinary place. After so long with only the hum of the wasp and the sound of the hoe hitting earth to fill his ears, he felt dizzy at all the new sounds . . . cattle grouching, geese complaining, loom rods rattling . . . doors banging, stones grinding, water sloshing. His eyes darted from one mud-baked building to the next, spotting more workers than he could possibly count. His head filled with words for what they were doing.

Here, women tore goat's wool into fine fibres, next

spinning them to yarn. There, men with multi-coloured arms stirred pots of dye. They slopped cloths in the stinking liquid, squeezing them out and setting them to dry on long wooden rollers. The sight of these vivid colours made Shabti look down at his own dirty kilt, then over to an airy shed where women were folding beautiful textiles of linen so fine even the weak fingers of sunset could push through them. His heart ached for the luxury.

More than the sights, it was the smells that turned him weak at the knees. Food! He was instantly giddy at the aroma of fresh bread baking in hive-shaped ovens. Even the scent of barley being crushed for new flour was faint but fantastic. Elsewhere lithe workers mashed fat grapes with their bare feet, the juices running out along stone troughs ready to be made into wine. Scum was skimmed off basins of fermenting barley beer. Fires crackled and stewpots bubbled as plump birds were plucked to be roasted. Mounds of fresh vegetables were chopped and spiced. Strips of fish meat dried in the late sun; pimply goose carcasses were trussed in rows, hanging from a wooden pole.

He remembered words for so many things – radishes, onions, leeks, cucumbers, cabbages, even strings of papery-skinned garlic. More – plums, carobs, cumin and coriander seeds. At this estate every kind of food seemed to thrive regardless of season.

Best of all, in one room, cooled by lengths of wet cloth at the doors and windows, a feast of fruit was being prepared. Dates were pitted and polished, figs split open to reveal their golden brown seeds and pomegranate flesh sliced and scooped into dainty bowls. It was agony to see juices dribbling down slivers of pinky-red watermelons, and to imagine the sweet flavour of the glossy apples. When he took a step closer, workers waved him away.

This feast wasn't for him.

He looked over to the high wall around the white house. No doubt whoever lived there would be gorging on a sumptuous meal very soon, but who was it?

He thought someone called his name and jumped to attention, afraid it was Master Hob again. All he saw was a cat, a stately tawny creature with golden eyes. The same cat that had been stalking in the river reeds? He put a hand to his face, remembering fur on his cheek just before he woke in the barley field. Beyond the cat, on the highest part of the house roof, a slender grey heron was drinking in the dying sunlight. For a moment he paused to do the same. The air was still so heavy he practically had to drag it into his lungs.

Failing to find anything that might be compost, he tipped his basket into a cattle pen. At the same time he looked enviously at the cows with their bales of food and troughs of water.

'Swap?' he asked whimsically.

In unison they turned away. He scooped a quick drink from the trough, trying not to gag on the scraps of straw floating in it. Perhaps there would be better food and drink at the Night House place he was supposed to go to? Would he even be able to find it?

Luckily, he spotted it just as the sun disappeared completely – a long mud hut with a flat roof, low doorway and absolutely no windows. One after the other, workers stooped and filed inside. He swallowed his nerves and followed the last man into the shadows. The colours were muted inside – sandy brown with dull red stripes. There was no furniture, just a solid bench of hardened earth backed up against each wall. Without speaking the workers moved into place and sat, legs neat, hands set on knees, eyes forward. Shabti copied them. He slipped his battered basket between his feet and set the hoe on his lap. It was the first time he'd stopped moving since waking in the barley field.

Night stretched out over the estate. Outside, workers in the compound moved by the dim light of smoky lamps filled with foul-smelling castorberry oil. Inside, the workers sat like statues. Shabti felt a million itches he wanted to scratch. Not least he wished he could swat the invisible wasp still buzzing near his ear.

Slowly, slowly, he wiggled his toes and stretched one leg out. Just as slowly he flexed his other foot. He couldn't keep quiet any longer.

'When's our turn to eat?'

No answer.

'How long do we have to stay here?'

Blank eyes.

'Where are we?'

Without interest or curiosity one worker slowly turned his head to look straight at the boy. '*Kemet*. This is Kemet. The black land.'

'But where are we? Where is Kemet?'

'Kemet is here.'

'Where is *here*?'

'Here is Kemet.'

'All right, I get that, but what about other places?'

The workers spoke in unison.

'*Deshret* is the other place. The red land. The bad land.'

Their ominous tone was enough to kill any further questions.

26

Shabti drew his legs up against his chest and wrapped his tired arms around them, resting his forehead on his knees. He slept.

The sound of a dull bell ringing split his dreams into a thousand pieces, all of them hissing like snakes. Instantly the other workers were on their feet, swaying slightly. As one they turned and faced the door. As one they marched out.

There was no sign of breakfast. The field workers walked with chins up and eyes forward as if refreshed and revitalized, while Shabti felt as limp as an old lettuce leaf. He absolutely couldn't manage another day in the sun without food and drink! Sneaking away to snatch a gulp of weak beer and an unguarded batch of bread rolls earned him five agonizing stripes from the whip and more blank looks from the other servants.

He was sent straight to the bean field again. Seeds sown at dawn were already sprouting leaves and growing tall. The weeds were just as healthy. Shabti couldn't bear another day wrestling them from the soil. How was it possible for the workers to keep going like this, without food or drink or proper rest? Why was he the only one with popping blisters and sun-sore eyes?

As before, the pattern of work followed the sun's

journey across the sky. At midday the plants were almost ripe, by late afternoon they were ready for harvest, by evening they were slumping to the soil. Once again he joined the line of workers to go back to the compound, barely able to lift his feet he was so exhausted. He was cheered up a bit by seeing the tawny cat. It was sunbathing on the flat roof of the dye shed, tail swishing and eyes winking. He winked back.

This pattern continued for . . . how many days? He lost count. There was no way to mark the passage of time, except by the sun's journey. His feet hardened. His skin peeled and grew tight around his bones. It didn't seem as if there could be any escape from drudgery by day and bad dreams at night.

One evening he was sullenly queuing to get back into the Night House, and, as ever, wondering how he'd fill his starving stomach, when suddenly he felt the ground shift and tremble. He wasn't the only one. A woman set down the wide tray of bread loaves she'd been carrying on her head. A man looked up from his work punching holes in a piece of leather. Two overseers gripped their whips, as if expecting trouble.

Nothing.

Yet.

The tawny cat crept round the corner of a hut where

fish were being gutted. It reached out one deft paw then scarpered, a fat silvery perch waggling from its mouth. Balance was restored. The compound settled back to a normal rhythm. Only Master Hob remained alert. He stood on a slight rise of land with Rip and Bite panting at his feet. The air flowing west from the red land of Deshret tasted of blood and iron. Instinct told him danger wasn't far away.

# 4 Just Rocks

*It was with a trembling hand that I struck the first blow . . .*
(Howard Carter, opening KV62, *The Discovery*
*of the Tomb of Tutankhamen*)

No more sky.

Going underground meant crouching like a crippled crab and somehow finding footing on the floor of a tunnel sloping downwards. Not fun with cracked ribs and other sundry sore spots. Dusty bulbs strung on loops of electric cables lit the way as daylight disappeared.

Jason warned, 'Watch your head on that bit there . . .'

'Where? Ow!'

Amy backed away from a rocky outcrop on the ceiling and pressed up against the side of the tunnel. Big mistake. The wall was coated in a nasty black powder. She tried brushing it off her clothes. Bigger mistake. The dust clouded up making her lungs wheeze and her eyes prickle.

'What is this stuff?'

'Bat droppings.'

'Bat dr— You've got to be joking?'

'Don't worry, there aren't any bats. Haven't been since Victorian times, when there used to be thousands of them nesting all over the west bank.'

'You're telling me this is *Victorian* bat poo? Great. How much further is it to the bottom?'

'Not far. It's a bit rough, I know. The ground underneath is a weak sort of shale that's really unstable when saturated with water. Tony says it's a miracle we even found the tunnel, there was so much flood debris dumped on top of it. The tomb's temple's long gone.'

Oh, so it was *Tony*, was it? Not Dr Clayton, or even Anthony, but chatty, pally-pally, we're-mates-on-the-telly *Tony*.

On cue, her dad's voice echoed up from below.

'Hallo, hallo? Is that you, Farouk? Is the X-ray lady here from Cairo yet?'

'It's me,' called Jason in reply. 'Farouk says Dr Hassan's going to be delayed a couple of days.'

'I'm here too,' Amy called down.

'Munchkin?'

She saw her dad come into view at the bottom of the

tunnel. From above he seemed squashed and squat. A nearby bulb created a spotlight's circle around him. How appropriate. She felt a bittersweet twist of love on her lips. Good old Dad, in a let's-play-Indiana-Jones hat, with his shirt straining over his belly. *Action Archaeology*!'s very own superstar. Her smile faded as she watched his eyes widen and his jaw almost unhinge with surprise.

'Amy! You look . . . different. I almost didn't recognize you. Last time I saw you, you were all pink and pretty, and here you are now . . .'

. . . still wearing black, even though the funeral was months ago.

Dad quickly popped a mint in his mouth – a trick she'd seen him do on TV whenever he needed to buy time before speaking. 'Come on down. Watch your head. Any problems with the flight? How's your mum? And Claire? Everything tickety-boo with my unborn grandson?'

'How'd you know it's a boy? And they're fine, except . . .'

'Of course it's a boy. Don't step on those cables. No room to swing a cat in here. Not that you'd want to – cats being sacred in ancient Egypt and all that.'

He breezed through introductions to Kev and Dez, the camera crew. Amy wondered what he'd already told them about her. Was it a trick of the light, or were they looking at her funny? People did, when they knew what had happened.

Her dad rushed through a history of the work so far. 'We're calling this the Chariot Tomb – though officially it's known as TT439. TT stands for Theban Tomb, since we're on the Theban west bank, like KV stands for Valley of the Kings, just over the ridge.'

'Except it doesn't, cos then it'd be VOTK, wouldn't it?'

'What? Oh, ha ha.'

Reluctantly Amy took off her sunglasses to look around. Despite the press of bodies and the shine of modern technology, the tomb was depressingly dreary. Not at all what she'd hoped to see – or what the famous Dr Clayton had boasted he'd find. Instead of fabulous paintings the walls were streaked with some sort of fungal infestation and stained smoky black in patches. It was also unbearably hot. She'd expected the chilly damp of English caves, not this oppressive underground oven.

'Never mind all the flood damage in here,' her dad cried out. 'Come on through to the coffin room!'

Jason began, 'We usually refer to it as a sarcophagus . . .' Then he paused. 'Are you OK, Amy? You look a bit freaked.'

'Sheer excitement,' she answered quickly, hoping he wouldn't wonder why she was wary of being face to face with a coffin.

Once through the squat doorway she only took shallow breaths and kept her eyes lowered. Just on the edge of visible she saw a young archaeologist hunched on the floor, sweeping a delicate brush over a sad patch of painted plaster. The woman wore combat trousers, clompy boots and a crumpled white T-shirt. She looked up at Amy and crammed corkscrews of dusty blonde curls behind her ears, dislodging two pencils and a pair of sunglasses.

'Hey, Amy. Good flight? How's things in England? Still raining I bet. Sorry,' the woman held out her hand, 'I should've said – I'm Ellie Powell. One of the field archaeologists.'

Amy's dad barged in on the introductions. 'A Yorkshire lass born and bred. *Ee bah gum* and all that.'

'Oh give over!' She rolled her eyes at Dr Clayton. 'Look, I'm almost done here if you want photos of the chariot rider. How about I have a nosy at that spot down the slope I was telling you about . . .?'

He frowned. 'Still banging on about your second-tomb theory?'

'It was just a hunch.'

'Hunch schmunch! Give me *facts* every time. Don't forget we only found TT439 because of scientific mapping of the wadi.'

Amy couldn't resist a sly contribution to the debate. 'Jason said some bloke called Farouk found it.'

He stared at her as if she were some sort of obscure artefact. 'Ah, well, Farouk's son's dog was digging around, if you want to be picky. Look, finish up here, Ellie, then give me a hand getting the coffin ready for its TV debut when the woman from Cairo *finally* arrives.'

He turned away, expecting Amy to follow, but she bobbed down to see what Ellie was working on. Nothing special. Just a patch of painted plaster about as big as two splayed hands.

'A chariot rider,' Ellie murmured as she delicately smoothed the brush bristles along the artwork. 'This is the wickerwork chassis – makes it fast and easy to manoeuvre in battle. I'd put it a couple of centuries after Tutankhamun, probably nineteenth dynasty. Here are the horses' feather plumes and decorated bridles. Shame the top of the picture's crumbled away.'

The chariot rider had no head. Amy could clearly see the lines of his fine pleated kilt though. He had one hand on the reins and the other pulled back.

She asked, 'Is he holding a whip?' and was strangely

pleased to see Ellie nod. Maybe the *Action Archaeology!* team didn't despise her in advance after all.

'Could be a whip,' Ellie agreed. 'I like this bit best, by the wheels. Two curling tails, possibly greyhounds. Noblemen used to hunt with them.'

Amy felt her skin begin to prickle. It could have been the heat, or her jumper rubbing. Or it could have been the sudden realization that the big stone box in the centre of the room probably contained the body of the chariot rider himself.

Barely breathing, she rose and took silent steps across the rough floor. She heard the speedy thump of her pulse and licked her dry lips. There it was, stark and solitary. Someone's last resting place.

The sides of the sarcophagus were carved with faint pictures. Dim electric light gave the red granite an eerie glitter. Without realizing it, her fingers reached forward to trace the images – goddesses with wings, deep-rimmed eyes and gods with animal heads. There was a thick crack across the centre of the sarcophagus lid. She found herself drawn towards the dark jag, even though she wanted to yank herself away. It was one thing to mess around joking about mummies – how many times had she said *ha ha* to girls at school who spent Halloween wrapped in loo roll and stomping around like homicidal zombies? Yes, joking about death was all very well, wearing black gear and plastic skulls was all fine and good, but this wasn't a joke or a fashion statement. It was real.

She leaned over the darkness to look inside, just as something reached out and grazed her shoulder.

Instinct kicked in.

The second Amy felt something touch her she jabbed her elbow back, *hard*.

Ah.

Not a murderous zombie mummy.

Just Jason, coming to join her by the coffin.

'Crap on a bike!' he gasped.

She watched him double up, vaguely pleased to have disturbed his equilibrium.

'Sorry, I thought you were . . .'

'What? A trained assassin? A killer whale? Where'd you learn to do that anyway – kung fu classes?'

'Primary school playground.'

'I didn't mean to scare you,' Jason said as soon as he got his breath back.

'I wasn't scared. It doesn't feel haunted here. More like . . . empty. Soulless.'

Ellie looked up from her work.

'The ancient Egyptians believed they each had more than one soul,' she said. 'One was the life-force, called your *ka*, the other was more like your personality – your *ba*. When you died the *ba* was supposed to fly as a bird, free to travel between the real world and the underworld as long as it could come back and be united with its body, otherwise it would die for ever . . . be utterly annihilated.'

'How exactly are you supposed to die *twice*?' Amy asked.

'The first time your body dies, you're not really dead, at least, your soul isn't. It goes off to fight your way through the underworld and be judged as good or bad.'

The idea of being judged made Amy squirm. 'So . . . what counts as bad?' she asked, thinking, *Bet I've already qualified, no problem.*

Ellie didn't quite answer the question. 'You're either worthy of afterlife paradise or wiped out for ever. That's the ultimate horror for an ancient Egyptian – being utterly obliterated. It's why there are so many hieroglyphs of people's names written everywhere, to keep the name alive. If your name's forgotten you're *nothing*. Extinctamundo for all eternity.'

'What's this guy's name, in the sarcophagus?'

'Sadly, no idea. Floods and fungus have destroyed all the writing that would have been on the walls. There could be a name somewhere in the mummy's wrappings. We'll know more when the expert arrives.'

'That X-ray scientist Dad's expecting from Cairo?'

Ellie smiled. 'Yeah, Dr Hassan. She's nice, you'll like her. We got introduced the first time I came to Egypt as an undergrad. She'll be doing X-rays and CAT scans.'

'It'd have to be someone rich,' Jason added. 'To get buried in a fancy rock-cut tomb like this.'

Rich? Not any more.

Amy didn't like the thought that a rich existence ended with a cracked coffin and bat droppings. That you could be so full of life then face death. Be utterly obliterated. Extinctamundo. Forgotten.

IN MEMORIAM . . .
WE WILL REMEMBER THEM . . .
IN LOVING MEMORY . . .

Words to try and keep a dead person alive.

*Except you can't!* she thought with a sudden intensity. *When they're dead they're* dead.

'You heading out?' Jason asked.

'Too hot!'

Somehow she made it out of the tomb and up the tunnel without major grazes or sprains. She scrambled a little way down the slope, skidded, stopped, skidded again;

more fell down than sat down. Pretended she'd meant it that way all along. White dust from the rocks added to the black dust of the bat dung.

The sun was at least lower in the sky, not as blistering as before. On the wadi floor the overseer, Farouk, was calling workers to finish for the afternoon. None of them glanced in her direction. Would anyone come looking for her? Long minutes passed. No one did. Fine. Let them stay cosy underground, chatting about dirt and damp and flood debris.

Tiredness finally caught up with her. So here she was after the long, long journey. Arrived. Stopped. Stuck all alone in a strange land. She checked her phone. No messages. So she stretched out. Didn't care about the lumps of rock in her spine and the gritty sand all around. Didn't care about anything. Let her eyes close. Became lost in the sensation of lying flat on her back entirely exposed to the sky. Sand slid down to stick on her kohl eyeliner. As she dozed she felt it tickling but couldn't be bothered to brush it away. One grain of sand. Maybe the same grain once blew into Cleopatra's eye, or got stuck between Tutankhamun's toes.

The desert loomed over her and the world turned tirelessly beneath. She was as small as the sand, and as unimportant. Earth, rocks and cliffs; she had a vision of the planet beneath her as one giant burial ground, turning in the vastness of the universe, the crust crammed with dead bodies. Time blew past like the breeze on a sand dune – endlessly changing, endlessly the same.

When she woke – had she even been asleep? – she felt the soft touch of fur on her cheek. Drowsily she brushed it off. Opened her eyes. Nothing there. A piece of rock jostled her hand. Idly she picked it up. It was white but not as crumbly as chalk. Limestone? There had to be thousands of fragments littering the wadi floor, presumably piled up when the tunnels and tombs were first excavated, or washed along by the improbable floods people kept mentioning. Nothing exciting. Just rocks.

Then she saw that this particular rock was smudged with something on the reverse. Lines. Pale brown lines deliberately drawn on the smooth surface. She almost dropped the stone in surprise. Looking up at her was a fluid cartoon of a curvy, clear-eyed cat.

Not any old cat.

This was a great tawny creature standing on its hind legs, looming over a row of little mice. There were faint squiggles in the top right of the sketch, disappearing over the broken edge. Hieroglyphs – the ancient Egyptian form of writing.

She stared at the rock in amazement. She'd seen enough episodes of *Action Archaeology!* to know that people didn't just find stuff like this lying around . . . it usually took months or years of planning and excavation to turn up ancient artefacts.

More marvellous still, the lines of the cartoon were so cleverly drawn that whichever way she turned it, the cat in the picture seemed to be looking right at her.

One front paw reached straight out and dipped down, as if pointing to the ground beneath her feet.

# 5 The Shady Garden

*May my soul rest on the branches of the*
*trees which I planted . . .*

(Tomb inscription *c.* 1400BC)

After another day in the sun, Shabti could hardly stand without the ground beneath his feet seeming to tremble. Worse, he felt as if some malevolent snake was in his gut, stealing whatever food he did manage to wolf down so he was always twisted with hunger. Other scaly creatures filled his nights with poisonous dreams. Somewhere in between these torments he found a quiet place in his mind. Here he nurtured resentment. Here he chanted the litany of, *This isn't fair! I don't deserve this!*

One evening he decided to go exploring. Unlike the other workers, content to sit as statues all night, he was crawling with curiosity about everything around him.

This place *Kemet* was familiar and strange at the same time. Why did he feel so horribly out of place? Why was he constantly battling the instinct to whip round and see if there was something behind him? Most importantly, why wasn't he the one living in the grand white house, wallowing in luxury?

He *had* to get back where he belonged. Wherever that was.

It was unpleasant to creep out of the Night House, grazed by the unblinking gaze of the statue-still workers. Keeping a lookout for dogs, he skittered through the shadows to where the pristine house wall was broken by a thick stone archway. The memory of a word surfaced. It was a *pylon.* The pylon was decorated with beautiful carvings, as was the wooden gate beneath it. He gave it a tentative push. It opened soundlessly. Quickly he slipped through the gap, under the pylon and into the mystery beyond.

Paradise!

Instead of hot, dry winds from the desert, the air was so fresh and beautiful he was instantly drunk on it. The wall enclosed a large garden cooled by a wide pool in the centre. Trees and flowers of every kind grew around the pool, separated by pathways of patterned tiles. The lush fruits and flowers were all shades of night-grey, but their scents were pure – roses vied with jasmine to cloud the air, mixed with perfumes of countless exotic woods. As he took his first steps around the garden he brushed past sleeping daisies, great frowsy chrysanthemums, cornflowers and poppies.

The inside of the high wall was literally loaded with vines and other trellised fruit trees. For a moment he thought he saw heavy snakes hanging down amongst the grape clusters. He blinked. Just twisting branches. Near the pond, papyrus plants spread their fan-like fronds, while on the surface of the water, sleepy lotus buds were jostled by the fat fish swimming underneath. He forgot all his fear to crouch at the pool and cup fresh water to his cracked lips. It tasted better than the richest wines, despite a lingering tang of waterweed. A little brown hedgehog came out of the shadows to watch him drink.

Why was this garden so wonderful, when outside everything was harsh? Why wasn't he allowed to live in luxury, instead of sitting in grisly silence with the other workers?

He brushed through a line of gentle willows towards the house. Open shutters showed squares of golden light and the elusive shapes of people moving about in the rooms inside. Lucky people. More than anything Shabti wanted to enter the house, to sink into a calm corner and have servants bring him every kind of food and drink – all the things he'd seen workers preparing out in the compound.

Not a chance of it.

Guarding the colonnaded step to the front door was the tawny cat with eyes that glittered even in the darkness. Shabti stopped dead, struggling to remember whether cats were dangerous. Surely not . . . ? He had no particular recollection of them, only of lean dogs racing at his side. The cat yawned. Its teeth didn't seem too savage. Shabti crept forward. The cat stared up at him.

'I just want to look,' Shabti whispered. 'I want to know who lives in the house.'

As if on cue, words came drifting from one of the open windows, carrying with them the scent of warm honey cakes and cinnamon spice. Shabti heard a girl's voice, so soft it only grazed the air. Then came Hob's deep growls. The girl was giving orders and the overseer was replying. It was satisfying to know that even the bullying Master Hob had to answer to someone . . . but who?

Just as Shabti began to tiptoe closer to an open window he heard a more sinister sound – the click of dog nails on a hard floor. The dogs Rip and Bite came out of the doorway, with Hob stomping close behind, his face as angry as a desert storm. The overseer stood for a moment with his arms folded, smelling the air as if he could sniff trouble. The dogs were already nosing through dark leaves to where Shabti had quickly hidden, round the far side of a sycamore tree. He knew they'd soon find him and drag him into the open. Whipping would probably be the least of his punishments for trespassing in such a special place.

Amazingly, Rip and Bite began to back away with white eyes and low-slung tails. What had scared them? Shabti almost squawked as something soft brushed his leg. It was the cat again! Having seen off two brutal canines, it calmly sat down and began to lick a dusting of pollen off one paw.

'Thank you,' he whispered, as soon as it was safe. The cat ignored him.

The girl's voice from the house called, 'King! Come here, King!' Only then did the cat leap to attention . . . and into the house through an open window.

Shabti smiled. He had a *king* on his side! Even if it was only a cat, it was comforting to know that not everything was against him.

Confident he'd soon find something to eat he turned to explore further . . . and promptly tripped over some kind of fluffy footstool stupidly placed on the path in front of him. He fell flat on his face. The footstool was in fact another cat, a ridiculously fat grey and white thing, with a belly so round it grazed the floor as it swayed.

'And thank *you* too,' he whispered sarcastically.

The cat butted him and purred. Shabti saw a glint of silver round its neck and caught his breath. White gold! Worth more than all other precious metals, more than spices and perfumes. Deep in his heart a snake of envy uncoiled and made him reach for the shiny collar. It was carved with two glyphs – picture words of the sounds *Ta* and *Miu*.

'Looks like I can read, even if I can't remember learning. Ta Miu, huh? *Lady Cat*. Bet *you* don't have to weed pea fields.'

Ta Miu rolled over on to her back with all four short legs waving in the air. Shabti let go of the collar and rubbed the cat's belly instead. Instantly clouds of loose fur tufted his hands and drifted in the air, clinging to his face and tickling him all over.

'Kind of you to share your sheddings, cat, but I can't eat fur, and it's not much good for anything else, is it?'

Ta Miu wriggled upright and began batting imaginary moths. Shabti sat on the path and tried to rub the fur from his hands. It twisted between his palms, making him think of the women turning wool into yarn; linen flax to thread. He pulled more fur from nearby leaves and added it to his twist. The daft cat had so much fur he was twirling it into string!

As he sat inadvertently spinning, little scamperings nearby caught his attention. King appeared again, trotting behind a line of tiny brown mice. It looked as if he were shepherding them along the path to a certain spot a few paces away. It was a strange way for a cat to play with prey – another peculiar thing about Kemet, perhaps.

With King watching over them, the mice began to nibble at nothing in particular – nothing but thin air, it seemed. *Stupid creatures*, he thought.

One mouse, bolder than the rest, scurried forwards until suddenly its wet nose, wide whiskers and bulbous black eyes were lost to view. Half its head disappeared! Reappeared again! The mouse whipped round and ran away . . . not quickly enough to escape King. One tawny paw caught the mouse's tail and held it still. The little creature quivered, its breath a mere tremble.

Shabti forgot all about hunger and thirst. He stared at the patch where the mice had been gnawing. He was still staring when a dramatic tremor made the ground ripple and leaves shake down from the trees . . .

# 6 Cats and Dogs

*There before us lay the sealed door, and with its
opening we were to blot out the centuries.*

(Howard Carter, *The Discovery of the
Tomb of Tutankhamun*)

*A*ction Archaeology! *History as it Happens! Live, on-the-spot
investigations, daily discoveries and dramatic finds . . . !*

Except *Action Archaeology!* weren't on the spot.

Only Amy Clayton was.

She glared at the cat on the flake of limestone.

*You're just a picture, cat, so stop looking at me like that. I
don't care if you're pointing at the ground. I'm not bloody
Howard Carter – don't expect me to start digging.*

The best thing would be to throw the cat picture away
– forget she'd even found it. At the very least, hand it over
to Dad, or Ellie, for them to gush over. Or let Jason writhe

with jealousy that she'd found something special and he hadn't. Certainly it would be complete madness to start pulling rocks away from a random spot on the ground just because of some hunch.

*Hunch schmunch.*

The sun dipped low over the cliff tops. She looked up, imagining she had seen something silhouetted against the burnt orange sky. Was it a dog? Could be. Or were there still jackals in Egypt? She'd read about jackals scavenging ancient cemeteries, along with human tomb robbers. Was that so far from the truth right now, when archaeologists were scarring the earth with their excavations into the dead ground?

The silhouette vanished. Nothing left to look at but cliffs, rocks and more rocks. Idly she pulled a couple of fragments away from a dip in the ground. Then a few more. It became quite compelling, like digging a hole in the beach that keeps on getting deeper but there's never an end to the sand. No one was there to film her. No one held a microphone near her mouth as she muttered, 'This is crazy, this is stupid . . .' Where was the *Action Archaeology!* team now? Where was crazy Clayton and his camera crew, introducing a new discovery . . .

The rocks came away so easily, almost as if something was waiting to be found. Barely half a metre into her accidental excavation she came across rocks that weren't lying carelessly scattered, but set vertically in front of her. No, not rocks, a narrow wall of pebbles jam-packed together. Nothing extraordinary in that. Absolutely nothing at all. No reason to wiggle round to her hands and knees to start digging again.

It was fun to pick at the pebbles and prise them free. It reminded her of the wallpaper in Grandma Clayton's spare room – nasty nicotine-stained woodchip. She'd spent many an idle moment lying on the lumpy bunkbed scratching at the flakes of wood embedded in the paper . . . earning Grandma's meanest disapproval. That was then, this was Egypt. Who'd mind if she messed about with a few more rocks? There was a whole desert of them after all.

One by one the pebbles fell away, revealing . . . a smooth whitish surface. No, not completely smooth. There was a pattern of horizontal arcs – sweeping, shallow lines. She stared at them, knowing they reminded her of something but not quite sure what . . .

*Oh my god!* (Where were the cameras to record *that* moment of realization?) It was *plaster*! She ought to have guessed it straight away. Hadn't she come to Egypt to escape from the dust of professional plasterers, who were redecorating her sister Claire's old bedroom to transform it into a nursery?

'What colour shall we do it?' Claire asked.

'Paint it black,' was Amy's immediate suggestion.

So Claire had plumped for lilac, saying that'd be a perfect compromise since she didn't yet know if she was having a girl or a boy.

Amy squinted at the plaster she'd inadvertently uncovered thousands of miles away from the new baby's room. Did this mean she'd found a wall? Since when were walls only about a metre wide? Why would a wall be topped by what looked suspiciously like a horizontal piece of wood?

She squinted and tried to imagine what Dad or Jason would see. The shape of her discovery didn't change, but she suddenly understood what it was. A door frame.

Impossible. Why would anyone build a door in the desert? Oh. Of course. For a tomb. It couldn't be a tomb. Jason said they were supposed to have temples, and there was no sign of one. Except it might have been destroyed, like the one belonging to the Chariot Tomb. Why wasn't there a tunnel, then? Maybe the tunnel got filled in by floods or whatever, or the roof cracked. This was definitely a door and what else would it be for out here in the middle of bare, barren, boiling nowhere?

She reached forward to graze the plaster surface with her fingertips. Even this slight contact made her hand tingle, as if mildly electrified. She rooted in her pocket and pulled out the cat drawing for reassurance. The cat's paws were still pointing straight at the spot where she was digging. Purely coincidental! Purely the way the rock was lying!

The sun dropped deeper with every minute. The sun set in the west, like life going out. The west was where life ended, so the *west bank* was where the dead were buried . . . underground . . . behind sealed doors. Secret for thousands of years until . . . until someone found them again.

Her conscience squirmed like a bowl of worms. She didn't need to be an archaeologist to know it was best to leave well alone – to go and get help. Yeah, get Dad, so he could pounce on something else sensational and ignore her some more. Get Jason so he could have extra star-time on telly.

Why should they hog all the action?

As the angle of light changed, she noticed a couple of strange markings on the plaster – oval ridges and whorls. Once again she reached out, this time fitting her own fingers over the shapes. She nearly fainted at the realization that she was touching *fingerprints* – dirty ones at that. Marks left by God only knows who as the plaster dried on the doorway and the . . . and the *what* sealed inside? She shivered. Something about the solemnity of the place kept her rigid. It was as if time itself had been embalmed, preserved for a long, long moment while she stared at the fingerprints.

How could she possibly see a door without wanting to know what was behind it?

No, she definitely wouldn't open it.

Just as she turned to scramble away, a streak of darkness came hurtling straight at her across the wadi floor – black skin, yellow eyes, white teeth. She froze. Didn't breathe, didn't move. Didn't even manage to scream. She *hated* dogs. Grandma Clayton had three nasty little yappers with bad breath and overactive bowels. 'Lovely doggies!' she'd croon. 'Come to Granny and get a cuddle. Ooh, you little slobberers, that's right, give Granny a kiss!'

This dog wasn't the cuddling sort. It bounded above her on the slope and sent sand and rocks skittering down on her feet.

Amy's mind jerked from one fear to another . . . *God those teeth are sharp. They'll hurt like hell then I'll catch rabies and die . . . How long will it take? Will it be agony? Can't I just be dead now and get it over and done with?*

Saying 'Nice doggie' wouldn't fool anyone. Looking around for Farouk or any other workers was pointless.

The wadi was deserted. The only people nearby were the archaeologists underground and any ancient bodies as yet disturbed in their rocky silence.

Slowly Amy began to back away from the semi-submerged door. The dog's growl deepened. She stopped. So did the growl. Stepped away . . . and was promptly yipped back into place.

*What, you want me to stay here?*

As if in answer, the dog dropped to its belly, paws stretched out, head up and ears forward like some sort of ancient monument. If it hadn't been panting with its tongue hanging out, she might have imagined it was an ebony statue.

She almost laughed. 'You look like Anubis, you know that? The jackal-headed god of the dead.'

Tentatively she crouched low, mostly thinking she could keep her body better protected that way if Anubis sprang. He didn't. He wagged his tail. When Amy sat right down and wrapped her legs close to her body, the annoying animal actually jumped up and skidded into the shallow dip with her, so close she could count his bony ribs. She closed her eyes and pulled her hands deep inside her sweater. Where would he bite first?

There was no biting. With an impatient bark, Anubis began to scrape at the door with one paw. Since it didn't look as if the dog had appeared with the express intention of tearing her throat out or chewing her fingers off one by one, Amy picked up a chunk of limestone and began to attack the top left corner of the door. The plaster crumbled easily. It fell away in dusty pieces, revealing another layer of rocks even more tightly packed than the first. It was no use telling herself to stop or mentally arguing that she was wrong, wrong, wrong. *Chip*, *chip*, *bash*. She rapidly perfected the crudest kind of technique for breaching the door. Then the moment came. The sounds of rock on rock changed subtly. One more knock and she'd be through. Curiosity was king.

Stop. Wait. If she broke through into an underground space, shouldn't she have a naked flame to test and see if the air was OK to breathe? Dad said fire would only burn if there was oxygen. Tough luck. No matches, no candles, no flames.

She took a deep breath in and held it.

One last bash and a hole appeared in the plaster.

Was it safe to breathe yet?

She did anyway, and so did the dog.

No sudden death.

Relief was followed by an excruciating urge to see what was beyond the hole.

Nothing.

Nothing there. Just an empty underground space.

She found herself leaning closer and closer, like leaning on the edge of an endless night without stars. Then the darkness was suddenly weakened by a glimmer of light as elusive as the patterns inside eyelids just before sleep. What happened next made Amy hold her breath for so long she nearly passed out.

Looking right back at her from beyond the hole were two eyes. Two glittering, golden eyes. One of the eyes slowly but surely closed. It winked at her.

# 7 Through the Hole

*It happens sometimes that hidden things, which in
themselves are easy to find, escape detection because
no one thinks of looking for them.*

(Amelia B. Edwards, *A Thousand Miles Up the Nile*)

As the ground began to tremble the evening air was
sucked away by a wave of wind streaming over the
whole garden, causing songbirds to wake suddenly. They
shot into the air calling, *Fear! Foes! Flee!*

Shabti staggered as the ground shook more violently.
Was it another hippo running past?

No! This time the whole world seemed to shudder.
Stars flashed like firecrackers. Cracks pushed up into
every mud wall and zigzagged across the hard earth of
the compound floor. There were crashes and thumps as
looms tipped over, pots fell to pieces and a thousand odd

59

items were shaken out of place. Now the cattle really were bellowing their unhappiness. The geese stretched out their necks to hiss at an imaginary enemy and every bird in the fields or marshes flew up as if a hundred hungry hunters were on their trail. Out beyond the river, in the red lands of Deshret, teeth gnashed and metal clanged . . .

The earthquake even dared disturb the sanctuary within the high walls of the garden. Some trees lurched at strange angles. A decorated seat shaded by an arbour of flowers cracked right down the middle. A few slatted wooden shutters were jostled loose from their hinges.

Shabti scrambled towards the gate. He felt his very bones clattering as the vibrations dwindled and things slid back to normal. A heavy silence then muffled the compound, broken only by the sudden high chime of a silvery bell ringing from the white house. A feathery voice called for help.

Overseers sprang up to shout orders. Slowly workers shook off the dust and waited to be told what to do. Some came staggering from the ruins of collapsed huts. Other figures were motionless under piles of rubble. They wouldn't be moving again. Trembling, Shabti tore his gaze away from the sight of scattered goods and shattered bodies.

He hid in the shadows again, not a moment too soon. Hob and his dogs headed straight back to the white house, followed by workers with lamps and tools. They didn't waste a moment looking at the starlit beauty of the garden; never even troubled to notice the night-time perfumes.

Was this normal then, this world-shaking calamity? Surely not. Shabti could easily sense a new urgency in Hob's orders. Was it some kind of attack from Deshret? All the more reason to escape, forget the earthquake, find a way out of Kemet.

He turned back to where the invisible hole had been. Ta Miu was long gone and the mice had scattered, but King was still there, crouched low with his long tail swishing from side to side. The cat watched as the boy lay flat on the ground and blew into the hole. Warm air seemed to flow out of it.

*I can't see it but I know it's there . . .*

Hidden in the shadows, he began by pushing things through, not his finger at first, he was too cautious for that. He picked an elegant green willow leaf and watched the tip disappear into the hole, then reappear as he pulled it out again. He tried the same action from the other side of the hole and found that the leaf vanished and returned looking no different. He uprooted a long purple iris and pushed that through next. It too disappeared into the hole. It fell when he let it go and there was no way of telling where it landed. Next he pulled a bendy willow switch off the tree, feeling a bit guilty at the scar he left behind. He marvelled at how the hole swallowed it, then gave it back again, unchanged. Which was all very well, but how was he supposed to work out how deep the hole was? What he really needed was a length of rope . . .

He looked down at his kilt and wondered about unravelling a length of the linen thread. He didn't fancy making the strip of cloth much shorter than it already was, but it was in a good cause . . . Then he noticed the twist of Ta Miu's fur lying on the path where he'd dropped it.

'Hey, puss, d'you want your belly rubbing again? C'mon, puss – puss, puss!'

Forgetting the trauma of the earthquake as only a fuss-loving cat can, Ta Miu came bounding out of the undergrowth. Very soon Shabti had a fluffy cloud of fur to work with. He tried to remember how the women had spun their flax and wool. Hadn't they had some kind of stick with a weight on? There was no time to think about filching one of those. He didn't know how long he had before the world convulsed again, or, worse, Hob came looking for him. There was no time to worry if what he was doing was possible or not. He couldn't wait to find out what the rules of Kemet were – he wanted to make rules of his own.

Rule One: look after self and escape.

He sat down by the hole and began to twist the fur with his finger ends, licking them to help the process. It was amazing how easy it was to turn the long, soft fibres into a kind of string; even more amazing to test the string and feel how strong it was.

'Nice work, kitty. Now wobble over there while I drop this inside the hole . . . Maybe I could tie a pebble on the end to weight it . . . No, stop playing with it, Miu! It's not a toy.'

He fed the thread through the hole, all the way in. It didn't snag and he couldn't hear the pebble knock against anything. He measured the string along his arm once he'd pulled it out again. It went round his thumb and elbow twelve times – there must be a long drop on the other side of this mysterious hole. Too far for a boy to jump?

'That's not the biggest problem,' he murmured. 'I still don't know if it's safe for me to go through . . .'

As if in answer King slipped away into the shadows of a chrysanthemum bush, while Ta Miu came to have her warm ears scratched. When King next appeared he was holding a tiny brown mouse gently between his jaws, perhaps the very same one he'd caught earlier. He dropped the mouse at Shabti's feet. It didn't run away or hide, just waited, completely still. Shabti reached out and touched it, feeling it tremble. Well, he did want to know if something could live on the other side of the hole. Was it right to put the mouse through? The dark part of his heart shrugged the question off – who cared what happened to anyone or anything else? The thing that mattered was to do whatever he could to get away to a better place. He was certain he didn't want to spend another day in the fields, in the compound, even in this wonderful garden. More than his fear of Hob, the dogs and the horrible hard work, he was anxious to slough off the sensation of being followed; the idea that something was lurking a little way behind him, waiting to pounce. If this hole meant freedom, then he'd use it.

He squashed his conscience flat and tied the fur string round the mouse. He put the little creature through the hole and let the string drop.

The mouse only squeaked as it fell. Quickly Shabti pulled it back out of the hole and into fresh air. It sat on his palm and immediately set about cleaning its whiskers. Its beady eyes seemed to say, *Finished with me yet?*

'I suppose I am.'

He set the mouse on the ground and it happily scampered away before either cat could decide to have a playful swipe.

Time for something more daring. Time to feel inside the hole himself.

Ta Miu purred encouragingly as Shabti put his fingers into the hole and gave them a wiggle. Was it warmer through the hole? Hard to tell. He put his whole arm in, right up to the shoulder, waving it from side to side. At first he felt only air, then he jumped in shock as his hand knocked against something hard. It took a lot of courage to keep his arm in the hole for more blind explorations. He thought he could have found a wall. It was quite smooth and a little bit powdery. When he pulled his arm back out of the hole he saw that there were faint traces of colour on his fingertips. A painted wall, perhaps. Only one way to see for sure.

He widened the hole. It seemed to stretch quite easily, despite the fact he couldn't see or feel it at all. Taking a deep breath, he put his head inside. He was glad to have Ta Miu sitting on his foot as a kind of emotional anchor, even if the cat was uncomfortably heavy.

What did he see?

Nothing. It was too dark.

That problem was readily solved by sneaking up to the house and quietly 'borrowing' one of the lamps carelessly left on the porch. It was a hand-held clay lamp with a piece of linen pushed into the spout for a wick. The kikki oil inside wasn't the best quality – it was only for servants' use after all. It smelled nasty as it burned. Shabti didn't care about that. The warm lamp went through the hole first, its light promptly disappearing from the garden. Then he peered in.

It took a while for his eyes to adjust. The lamp hardly cast a wide circle of light, just enough to see vague outlines and dull colours. There was a room, definitely a room, with no apparent ceiling, but four walls – one of them near the hole – and a floor absolutely crammed with things. At first he was terribly disappointed. It was just a storeroom! A nicely decorated storeroom, true, but nothing better than a glorified cupboard, to be brutal. There were rows of pottery jars with wax seals, baskets with food and grains, boxes and bundles, a bed, a chair and other things too indistinct to be identified. Who cared about that? Shabti almost cried he was so upset.

Then he heard something, actually heard a sound inside the store, and he saw, or thought he saw, a river of small rocks sliding down the far wall. When a light flashed through he was so startled he stupidly dropped his lamp. It fell on to a pile of boxes and the wick went out. Before he could worry about how to retrieve it, he felt sharp teeth nipping at his left leg.

'Ow! Get off, cat!'

He backed out of the hole and was just about to start shouting at Ta Miu when he realized she'd been warning him. Rip and Bite were a few steps away on the path. Just behind them Master Hob came into view, and he had his whip uncurled. There was nowhere to run.

# 8 Wonderful Things!

*Surely never before in the whole history of excavation
had such an amazing sight been seen as the light
of our torch revealed to us.*
(Howard Carter, *The Discovery of the
Tomb of Tutankhamun*)

Anubis vanished into the twilight as voices came curling out of the tunnel to the Chariot Tomb. Dad was on his way up. He'd see what she'd done. Know she was guilty. The night wasn't yet dark enough to hide her.

Amy got to her feet and awkwardly began brushing her clothes down. As the voices got louder, it seemed as if the cliffs loomed higher and the very shadows reached into the wadi to point at her. Accuse her.

Her dad exploded into reality with a cheery grin and a wave. 'Amy? There you are! Ready to roll on back to the hotel? The grub's fantastic, you'll love it. Bet you're ready for bed, eh? Long journey!'

Ellie Powell had sharp eyes. She caught hold of Tony Clayton's arm and pointed.

Amy tried backing away from the hole. Rock fragments underfoot sounded painfully loud.

'There was a cat,' she said weakly. 'I mean, a dog. Anyway, I didn't do anything. I found it like that. At least, I poked it a bit but it wasn't my fault, I was just waiting for you guys.'

*In trouble again.* She tensed, ready to be dumped with another load of blame. But as soon as her dad realized the significance of the hole in the ground he switched roles and became Dr TV Expert.

'Kev? Kev! Camera! I think we've got something. Hurry up, the light's almost gone! I said, camera! We are supposed to be *Action Archaeology!* aren't we? Get a shot of me coming down the slope from the Chariot Tomb. Can you get a wide sweep of the sunset while you're at it? Amy, love, just step a little way right . . . that's it, out of the shot. All right . . . Quiet everyone! Silence of the grave!'

Amy was impressed how her dad could gush and walk at the same time. In a few hyperbolic sentences about twilit mysteries and sudden discoveries, he was crouching in the shallow dip and looking at the plastered doorway. At the hole. Then he stopped talking. He waved one arm behind him, signalling for Kev to pause the camera.

'Bloody hellfire,' he murmured. 'We really do have something here. Fancy you stumbling over it, Amy, when you don't even know anything about archaeology.'

She opened her mouth to object. Hadn't she listened to him read aloud his *entire* book manuscript, *Me and History*? True, she'd been trapped in bed with tonsillitis at the time, and hoping Dad would read *The Princess Bride*, like in the movie. Even so . . .

Jason got in before her. 'This is absolutely amazing! I know the Chariot Tomb was good to film, but this is, like, *real*. It's properly *Action Archaeology!* I can't believe we've actually got a new discovery.'

'It's not *your* discovery,' Amy said.

'Well, our discovery.'

'Ours?'

Her dad said, 'Ssh, Amy! I'm trying to see what we've got here. A tomb, I think. Definitely a tomb, or the antechamber to one.'

'So much for *hunch schmunch*,' Ellie murmured. 'Tony, shouldn't we get Farouk up here? Fence the area off so we don't compromise it any more?'

'No!' Dr Tony Clayton straightened up to his full

height. Ellie was still taller, so he pulled rank instead. 'I'm Field Director on this excavation and I'm quite happy for us to have a, er, a little look. So we can plan a proper analysis later, of course.'

'But we don't know how stable the slope is. There's a big layer of very weak shale under this slope of the wadi. Maybe that's how come this find has been exposed. It could be unsafe.'

'You mean the ground's sagged and the original tunnel to the tomb collapsed?' Jason asked, sounding as smooth as if the camera was actually on him.

She nodded. 'The Chariot Tomb is built right at the bottom of that deep fissure in the cliff there. Flash floods would have been channelled through it and down this slope, causing a lot of erosion. And instability.'

Clayton was too excited to take Ellie's concerns seriously.

'Don't be such a wuss,' he snorted. 'Farouk and his men have been lugging rocks down this slope for weeks and they never complained of instability. Now come and give me a hand making this hole a tad bigger. I think we can see inside. Wait a minute, the rocks are practically falling away anyway . . .'

He lay on his belly like a beached whale and put his face to the hole.

'Can you see anything?' Jason asked. Even the camera crew leaned in closer.

Ellie nudged in with more caveats. 'We should at least put the fibre optic camera in first . . .'

'Stuff that,' said Amy's dad. 'Give us your torch, Jason.'

Even with the electric light he couldn't get the right angle for peering into the hall. Then he yelped, just as Anubis had done.

'Blimey O'Riley!' he shouted. 'Kev, Kev, cameras again. Come low, level with my face. I want you to film me looking in. Ready? Let's go. *Here I am, on my belly like a snake, the only way to see inside through the breach in this doorway, a barrier that's remained close for – can we guess? – thousands of years, since the last worker plastered it over and walked away. The hole we've made is small, of course, so as not to disturb the integrity of the doorway. Shining my torch through I can see . . .'*

He paused, genuinely caught up in the moment.

What could he see?

*'Wonderful things! That's the only way to describe it, using Howard Carter's famous words from when he breached the door into Tutankhamun's tomb back in 1922, not far from this very spot. We've no way of knowing yet what will be beyond the door. Will it be royalty? Will it be robbed? I'm shining the torch through again, and there we have it. You can't see this at*

*home yet, but just imagine the scenes . . .*

'It's one of those magic moments when time seems to fold between one century or another, or could you even say time stands still? I'm peering into a rocky room. I can see square shapes and tall shapes. Boxes and bundles, piled right up against this very door. Just a few inches of rock separating me from ancient treasures! And the pictures! It's the most incredible view imaginable, things no one has seen until I shone the light through and looked in . . .'

He went on like this until Kev shook his head to indicate the conditions really were too bad to continue filming. Even then, Clayton couldn't stop talking. Amy tried several times to speak to him. When he finally heard her, her voice came out like a croak.

'What is it?' he asked.

'Nothing. I mean, I saw something too.'

'What's that? You looked in the hole? You shouldn't go doing things like that unless you're an archaeologist.'

'I still saw something.'

'What?'

'There was a cat. It had golden eyes. It . . . looked alive. Like it was winking.' The memory didn't seem so strange now that the new night was closing in on them.

'Winking? Don't be daft!'

Daft? Fine. If that's what he thought . . .

Then Ellie asked, 'Did you say winking, Amy? No, come on, Tony, don't scoff. It's not such a crazy idea. Remember the rest of Howard Carter's account of looking into Tut's tomb? He said drafts of air dislodged flakes of gold paint from the eyes of statues inside. It did look as if they were alive, as if the eyes were glittering.'

Amy's dad took off his hat and wiped a dusty handkerchief across his meagre streaks of hair. 'Yes, oh yes, that's right, I suppose. Well, gold is nice, eh? *Everywhere the glint of gold*, to quote Mr Carter.'

Happy that he'd recovered his prestige, he signalled for Ellie to come closer.

'Put your hand in and see if it is empty space.'

'Put my hand in *there*?'

'Go on! You're a sturdy Yorkshire lass, aren't you? Not afraid of the dark.'

'Maybe there are snakes,' said Jason suddenly. 'Farouk said you still see the *naja haje* on the west bank.'

Amy shuddered. Thank God she hadn't imagined snakes when she had looked into the hole. 'What's the *naja haje*?' she asked, even though she didn't exactly want to know the answer.

'The Egyptian cobra.'

'Is it venomous?'

'Oh yes!' Jason said. 'Deadly, like the Egyptian viper, or

the king cobra . . . God I *hate* snakes.'

Amy wasn't especially bothered by snakes, but she certainly didn't want to put her hand into a darkness that might be writhing with them. Neither did her dad, for all his Indiana Jones pretensions.

'Hey, Ellie, your hands are smaller than mine,' he said, clearing a space for her by the door. 'Judging by the state of this plaster, this door's been sealed for centuries. There won't be any snakes.'

Jason couldn't shake off his anxiety. 'Doesn't Farouk have a dog, to chase them off?'

Ellie said, 'Cats are traditionally good snake catchers. Think of the famous illustration from the *Book of the Dead*: the cat with the knife beheading the great Serpent of Chaos.'

'Better still,' he shuddered, 'let's *not* think of snakes.'

Amy was pleased to see there was something that could rumple his confidence. Then her dad yelled, 'Jason, Ellie, one of you! Get over here and reach inside!'

Watching the *Action Archaeology!* team bicker, she was reminded of the clockless twilights after school, when she was little . . . Stretching out the hours before bedtime with Claire and the other kids in the street . . . hearing the dull thud of a football being kicked about, the skid of bicycle wheels. That was the time when parents, rules and authority all slid away; when conscience couldn't keep them from little crimes – banging yard gates, smashing up a few bottles, trying to get a bonfire going. Amy smiled to remember her first and only bit of graffiti. AMY WOZ ERE carefully written in indelible black ink – her name immortalized for as long as the brick lasted.

Now the archaeologists were drunk on the same timeless half-light. Their eyes were bright with an excitement that outshone common sense. Ellie resisted as long as she could. Her lips were a thin white line of disapproval as she approached the doorway. 'Seriously, shouldn't we do a proper site analysis first? Take photos? Record everything?'

Amy's dad didn't even blink. 'It's OK, we're not filming. Come on, Ellie, this is what it's all about. It's telly after all. We're not doing anything *illegal*. You know we'll get round to sifting debris, doing a site survey, sorting conservation – all that blah. There are some boxes right up against the door. See if you can touch something.'

*Something's going to happen*, Amy thought, with sudden dread. *I don't want to be here. Don't want anything to do with anything. I'm just a tiny dot on the edge of everything spinning round and round . . .*

Jet lag. This horrible disorientation had to be tiredness. Her body remained on the spot, as if fastened to the ground with roots of stone. Watching Ellie stretching her bare arm into the hole was like being forced to sit through a horror movie . . .

'There are boxes,' Ellie grunted. 'I can feel the wood – ow – and the splinters. Hang on, one of the boxes has a loose lid. I think I can . . . Got it! It's hard and cool to touch.'

Gently, gently she pulled an object through the hole. Immediately Amy's dad snatched it from her and pushed it in front of the camera . . . which Kev set to play again, using torchlight for impromptu lighting.

'*Dragged across time, the first of many wonders from this marvellous new discovery. Here we have a beautiful blue jar patterned with lotus flowers, no longer lost from view but brought into the light for you to admire, just as some ancient Egyptian no doubt admired it several centuries ago.*'

Ellie withdrew a second object from the darkness and cupped it in her palms. Something made Amy go closer to see better.

It was a clumsy clay lamp, still stained with oil and haunted by the ghost of a long-lost scent. Was it olive oil? No, nastier. Cod liver oil?

As if reading her mind Ellie said, 'It might once have been filled with castorberry oil, called kikki oil in ancient times. It can't possibly smell after all this time. We must be imagining the stink.'

She passed the lamp to Amy, who almost dropped it. 'Dad! Look at this! It still feels warm.'

Her dad looked up, nodded kindly then returned to the exquisite blue vase. 'Just a lamp,' he said.

Just a lamp? Didn't he think it was amazing that an object from the past could look so real? So *immediate*?

A piece of blackened wick still protruded from the spout. It was as if the light from the lamp had only just been snuffed out.

# 9 Prisoner

*Get back! Crawl away! Get away from me, you snake!*
*(Book of the Dead)*

Hob hadn't even left him a lamp. Shabti watched the sun rise, shine and disappear, all beyond a small square window high in his prison wall.

It wasn't meant to be a prison. The floor of the room showed signs that it was sometimes used for storing cattle feed and maybe baskets of dried food. Shabti searched every bit of dust for odd grains to eat. His lips were starting to crack again he was so thirsty. How long would Hob keep him locked up?

Outside he heard the sounds of life in the compound. They were almost familiar to him now. He imagined the other workers setting off for their chores just as they always did . . . except they now had to walk past signs of earthquake damage. Familiar but *not quite right*, that was how things seemed.

He trailed his fingers around the four bare walls of the room. Had he been here before? No. Not this exact place. Somewhere like it then? Maybe. When he squeezed his eyes shut he almost remembered rooms, objects and faces, moving as if behind a gauzy curtain. Or were they just glimpses of things he'd seen through the windows of the white house? Why did he feel a powerful urge yanking him back there, as if there was something he needed to do?

Because it was better than baking in a mud hut, that's all.

'I wasn't doing anything wrong!' he'd yelled as Hob literally dragged him out of the garden, through the tall gates and back into the compound. 'I was just looking. *Let go of me!*'

Hob only laughed. His grip was so tight Shabti now had deep black bruises all along his arms. His fists hurt from slamming them against the door, demanding it be opened *at once*. His bare feet were sore from kicking it. His head was full of ideas for how to punish Hob once he had the chance. Whipping would be too good for the man . . .

His resentment never faded, but common sense soon

asserted itself. He had to figure out what to do next. What did he know about Kemet? How would that help him escape? There'd been a white hippo. No, before that, a barley field. No, first there had been fur brushing his cheek. Cat fur? Then the running, the river, the crocodile, and the glare of the bare red lands of Deshret. Hob had found him, made him work under some kind of spell. Work, pain, blisters, these were all new things, only, if he wasn't used to working, why had he woken up with a hoe and a basket?

Fine. If he couldn't understand why he was there, he could at least find out *where* he was. An oasis of plenty in the middle of a desert land, that's what it seemed to be. Everything the workers did, everything they ordered or grew or made, it was all for the owner of the white house. That had to be someone important.

*I'm important too*, came a stubborn voice in his head. It was enough to make him angry again. Yes, he would escape! The hole in the garden was the key . . . the hole down to that room with the shining gold eyes. If he could just get back to it and try again . . .

He broke his fingernails trying to gouge round the hinges of the door locking him in. What was the use anyway? Outside, Rip and Bite were splintering cow bones. They'd probably be happy to chew human marrow. Shabti wondered what else they'd eaten, out on the edges of the red lands. Master Hob had, at first, accused him of being a monster from Deshret. He wasn't . . . was he? He had arms, legs, hands, feet, a face, like all the other workers. Only he wasn't like them, not really. He needed to eat, to sleep, to drink, to pee – all things other workers never did. One thing more. He was better. He knew it, deep in the bones the dogs would gnaw on, he knew he was superior.

In the far corner of the room something stirred as he thought this. A shadow uncoiled.

'Who's there?'

His voice came out as a croak, not because he was scared, but because his mouth was so dry. That's what he told himself, even as his bones began to shake with fright.

'I said, *Who's there?*'

Too dark to see. The room had been empty before, hadn't it? Nothing had come in through the window, he was certain of that. There couldn't be anything there.

'You're just a shadow.'

The shadow hissed.

Shabti backed against the door.

The shadow seemed to grow larger.

82

'There's nothing there!' he shouted this time. 'You're nothing!'

The shadow rose up.

On the other side of the door Rip and Bite began to bark like mad things as Shabti banged on the wood and hollered to be set free. Was he imagining it, or was the shadow almost upon him when he heard Master Hob's hateful voice? The dogs were ordered to be silent and the bar on the outside of the door was lifted up. Shabti rushed out, straight into Hob's grasp. At that moment he didn't care. He would rather be whipped than face the brooding thing behind him.

'It's after me,' he cried. 'And I didn't do anything!'

With his free hand Hob flung the door wide open. 'What's after you, dunghead? The place is empty.'

'There was something in there!'

'Look for yourself.'

Even though he struggled against the order to look, Shabti found his head swivelling round to face the prison. Hob was right. It was empty – just a dust-scuffed floor and four bare walls.

'I won't go back in there!'

'You'll go where I tell you to go,' Hob snapped. 'Right now, you're going to look lively and come to my lady's house with me.'

'The white house?'

'Ay, the white house. My lady has said she wants to see you.'

For a moment Shabti had a vision of luxury awaiting him – a soothing bath, an endless feast, a soft bed and servants with cool fans wafting. Hob's next words broke that fantasy.

'She wants to know what sort of scum has been lurking in her garden and *stealing* from her. After that she'll want to know what I recommend doing to *punish* you. I have to say, I've been giving that matter a lot of thought, haven't I, lovelies?'

Rip and Bite yipped their agreement.

Even Hob seemed subdued as he walked up the broad marble steps to the door of the white house.

'Wait here. Don't touch anything.'

As usual, Shabti found he had to obey. He was left in a small entrance hall. Through two screened doorways he got a tantalizing glimpse of the room beyond. The walls of the hall were painted a pale morning yellow colour with strips of floral decoration at the top and bottom. The floor was clean and cool underfoot. In fact, since walking through the door he realized it was the first time he'd been at ease since first waking in the barley field. There was absolutely no clue within the house of the hardships endured without. The only sound was the faint drone of a wasp in some close corner.

A servant appeared. Not one of the field workers, not even one of the burly servants from the compound. This was a woman with immaculate hair and skin, dressed in a long, brilliantly blue gown, with pretty beads at her ears and round her throat and ankles. Shabti could only stare. He never once blinked as this servant signalled for him to follow her into a wider entrance hall. Eight stands of gleaming ebony held vases of fresh flowers that filled the room with a dizzying cloud of perfume. This was all he had time to notice before they went between a row of beautiful columns, carved like pillars of bound papyrus and fanning out to support a painted ceiling.

They came to what he supposed was the heart of the house. It was a wide square room open to the sky at the centre, though covered with layers of sparkling gauze. Lamp stands were placed discreetly in the corners of the room for soft lighting. The alabaster lamps certainly weren't filled with common kikki oil. The air smelled sweet.

There was a single chair set between two of the four pillars in this room. He couldn't tell what sort of wood it was, but the arms were inlaid with opalescent mother-of-pearl strips and the feet were shaped like lion paws. There was a fur rug spread in front and a low stool to one side.

He stared hungrily at the chair. What would it be like to sit in such a seat, to nestle sore feet in that thick rug, to wave one hand and have servants fetch every kind of cooling drink, every sort of delicacy dripping with honey? The snaky greed around his heart squeezed a little more tightly. Then he noticed what was on the stool. A little smile twitched at the corner of his mouth. He recognized it straight away – it was a board game, one of his favourites. *Senet*, yes, he remembered the name. This set wasn't as fine as the one he saw in his mind. It was only wood and ivory, not gilded. Even so, the wood was well-polished and the little game pieces were charmingly carved in the shape of animal heads – frogs for one player and hedgehogs for the other. His fingers itched to move them and win the game.

No such luck.

The servant snapped her fingers and signed for him to kneel. Heart suddenly racing, he did so. He kept his eyes just high enough to see in front of him. First to enter the room was Hob, with his big sandals and scarred legs. Then came four tawny paws as King calmly trotted in and sniffed at a dish of fish fillets that had just been set down for him. He dragged the fish off the plate and under the fancy chair. There he proceeded to eat with great concentration and appreciation.

Next, the air seemed to ripple with the wafting of soft feathers. Shabti waited, not daring to lift his head. The sudden hush told him the lady of the white house had entered the room.

# 10 Pictures from the Past

*Our task was to leave nothing unexplored which might add*
*to the sum of our steadily growing knowledge.*
(Howard Carter, *The Discovery of the*
*Tomb of Tutankhamun*)

It was not a restful night. Amy woke, or thought she woke, several times. She had her own hotel room, but she certainly didn't feel alone. Someone was in the room with her, the same someone who kept her company through her dreams. Her nightmares. She heard rain. Didn't know if it was outside or just in her mind. Noisy drops fell on metal, skin and plastic.

Was that her phone ringing? Just as dawn broke the darkness a new sound trailed into her consciousness, some kind of lament, or was it a celebration? She fumbled on the bedside cabinet, failed to find a light switch, located her phone by touch. Flipped the lid. Winced at the bright photo set as her phone wallpaper.

No messages. No one was calling, except holy men in the mosques. The dawn call to prayer.

She burrowed further into the sheets. The photo stayed floating in her mind – Claire and Owen in the garden back home, looking luminous.

More sleep. More bad memories raining down on her, soaking everything to a gloomy monotone. Light twinkled. A nice light. A kind gold light. The glitter of a cat's golden eye. She dreamed some more, but this time there were no horrors, only cats chasing mice, or were the cats chasing time away so she could stay in bed just that little bit longer . . . ?

She finally struggled out of sleep hearing the comforting drone of a vacuum cleaner in the hotel corridor. Ah. It was Luxor. Egypt. She stumbled out of the shower and into a jumble of black clothes and accessories. Didn't dare open the door . . . didn't know where to go for breakfast. Padded on to the balcony instead.

Her third-floor room faced into a courtyard garden, presumably home to the hordes of birds that had bellowed out the dawn chorus. Wooden loungers surrounded a blue-bottomed pool. Jason Henderson was stretched out on one of them, eyes closed and hair tickled by leafy branches.

Oh well. Suffering his company was better than being completely abandoned. She found her way down to him.

'What are you doing?'

'Worshipping Ra. There's room for two if you don't mind being half smothered by bushes of winter jasmine.'

She dragged another lounger over the pink tiles and hunched on the edge of it. 'You mean Ra the sun god?'

'One and only. Shines by day, slaughters evil by night. Amun Ra is, *was*, the supreme deity round here.'

'So basically, you're *sunbathing*.'

'Exactly.'

'Don't you burn?'

'That's what sun cream's for, though I guess you've got enough tons of make-up on so the UV can't filter through.'

'Has everyone gone already?'

'*Already?* It's ten o'clock. Didn't you hear them leave? They were tiptoeing like elephants and saying *sssh* loud enough to wake up a mausoleum of mummies. They couldn't wait to get back to TT440.'

'Four Four what?'

'The new tomb. TT440. We were up talking about it half the night. You fell asleep.'

'Why didn't they come get me before they went?'

'They're only filming the initial survey of the area. They

don't need me to present anything.'

'Aw, didn't *Tony* let you tag along for your fifteen minutes of fame?'

'Actually, I said I'd stay with you,' he answered rather stiffly.

'Oh.' She hid behind her sunglasses. 'It's not so hot today.'

'It will be. Look how the sun's coming up over the tops of the palms there. You can see why people thought it was a big ball being pushed across the sky.'

'Like those scarab things?'

'You've heard about dung beetles then?'

'Funnily enough, there is a brain somewhere under all these *tons of make-up*. I know scarabs don't eat people and that they spend all their time rolling round balls of dried poo to lay their eggs in. When the eggs hatched and the babies came crawling out, to the ancient Egyptians it looked like life starting out of dried mud. Like Ra shining on seeds to make them sprout – which is why the scarab is sacred to Ra. *Not* my number one choice of looks if I was a god though.'

Jason smirked. 'You'd be a hedgehog. Possibly cute underneath the prickles.'

*'Prickles?'*

'Sharp ones. So, where'd you want to go today?'

91

'I don't care.'

'Thought you'd say that. I've decided we're heading over to the Valley of the Kings. We filmed a few scene-setting shots for *Action Archaeology!* there. It's my second favourite place in the world.'

He was obviously waiting for her to ask where his *first* favourite place was. So she didn't.

The Valley of the Kings was another dry place, dominated by a high pyramid-shaped hill and smothered in mounds of broken limestone. Well-trodden paths spread across the valley floor and insinuated into every deformed fold of the cliffs. These paths led to all the excavated sites discovered so far: KV1 to 63. Some tomb entrances were protected by low stone walls or banks of dusty sandbags. Standing under the cloudless sky it never occurred to Amy that these were actually flood defences. The only flood she saw was the inundation of visitors.

Japanese tourists stepped off their coach and trotted straight over to take pictures of her studded black gear before setting their sights on more historical scenes. A phalanx of Egyptian women in full veils clapped and sang their way from the car park into the valley. One of them waved. Amy waved back shyly, thinking it wouldn't be so bad to be in head-to-toe anonymity like that. Forty

Germans in fluorescent orange baseball hats were absorbed by the gaudy souvenir shops leading up to the ticket office. Then Amy spotted a round-bellied boy bounding over as fast as his too-long galabeya would let him. He held a stalk of stiff sugar cane, decorated at the top with shiny *Hello Kitty* stickers.

'Hey, Mazen!' Jason called and waved. 'Glad you're here today. Amy, this is one of Farouk's kids, Mazen. Mazen, this is Dr Clayton's daughter . . .'

Amy didn't mean to be rude. She was just staring at the dog that was running at Mazen's side. As soon as he saw her he started jumping up and down, yipping with excitement. She had to back off as he snagged claws in her droopy black sweater.

'*Yalla*, Anubis!' said Mazen.

'Down!' snapped Jason.

The dog licked Amy's chin once and returned to his owner.

'Is he really called Anubis?' she asked.

'After the Egyptian god of embalming,' Jason said.

'I *know*!'

Thinking it over, it wasn't such an extraordinary coincidence. An obvious name, even. Like calling a tabby cat Tiger, or a white one Snowy. Amy's cat was called Fat Lad, no prizes for guessing why.

Mazen tugged at her sweater. 'Hey, lady! Something shopping? No bloody hassle! Asda price! Cheap as chips!' He mimicked the other vendors brilliantly, then handed her a plastic pyramid paperweight. 'A present for you!'

'Er, thanks.'

Amy shook it and watched a storm of glitter rise around the scarab charm inside the pyramid.

He pulled on her sweater. 'You hot? Too hot?'

'I'm fine.'

'OK OK. You want to see Tut-tut? *Yalla* – come with me.' He pulled them past the many Egyptian men selling tickets and guarding tomb entrances.

'His brothers . . .' Jason murmured.

At KV62 Mazen led them to the bottom of a dirty flight of stairs.

With a shock Amy realized she'd walked right into the middle of one of her secretly-savoured books on Egyptian archaeology: she was standing on the very spot where Howard Carter first breached the door into Tutankhamun's tomb. It was impossible not to think of another doorway in another valley not so far away. What was Dad looking at? What were they filming? Her conscience prickled as she felt the limestone cat cartoon in her jeans pocket. She really had meant to give it to her dad, only the night before there never seemed to be the right moment. Now it was an insistent presence, tugging her attention away from the here and now, over to the discovery at TT440.

Mazen announced, 'I am Howard Carter!' He did a great pantomime of playing the famous archaeologist – stroking an imaginary moustache, hustling Lord Carnarvon and the other spectators out of the way, breaking through an invisible door and holding up a candle to peer inside.

'Won'ful things!' he ended with a bow.

A cluster of tourists pushed past him, coming out of the tomb. Amy heard them complain: *Very small. Disappointing. Not much treasure left. Can't see what all the fuss is about.* They reminded Amy of Charlotte Pratt, who always swept through school as if she was meant for better things, or as if there was a bad smell in the air. These tourists were probably keen to get back to their cruise boat for yet another meal and a spot of Ra-worship.

Mazen watched Amy's eyes brighten as she stepped into the set of rooms that had once been crammed with Tutankhamun's treasure.

There was a bare antechamber about the size of her bedroom at home. This would have been stuffed with objects needed in the afterlife, as well as a smaller treasure chamber and a store room. The actual burial chamber was pretty small too. She couldn't imagine how the massive golden sarcophagi had even been assembled inside the room, let alone fetched out again by Carter's team. The boy king's last gold sarcophagus was all that remained. It looked starkly alone. All the other wonders had been taken to the Egyptian Museum in Cairo.

She stared at the spotted mustard walls with the rows of baboons and other strange images. Was this what it had been like in the ruined Chariot Tomb? Was this the sort of thing they would find in the new site, TT440? It was unsettling, the fierce pull she felt towards a place she'd only glimpsed for a few seconds.

Mazen was a brilliant guide. He took them into so many tombs in the Valley of the Kings that Amy soon lost track of how many tunnels she entered, how many steps she climbed and how many colours she marvelled at. Some tombs had high ceilings, columns and several chambers. Some were so small they quickly felt crowded. Everywhere they went guides cried, 'No photo! No photo!'

'The flash damages the colours,' Jason explained. 'The tombs are already suffering enough just from us breathing inside them. It makes the air too moist.'

Mazen pointed out his favourite pictures – the ones of Anubis, of course, presiding over judgement of the dead. In each tomb Jason looked for the god Ra, whose bold sun symbol was everywhere. He found several pictures of

Ra's solar boat, which took lucky souls on their final journey to immortality. He also showed her scenes from the Egyptian underworld, a place called Duat, which had twelve gates – the twelve hours of night – each guarded by a fearsome demon. Jason was particularly repelled by the coils of the Serpent of Chaos. He passed this picture quickly and pointed out a scene of judgement in the underworld. Here a grotesque deformity called Ammut the Devourer squatted.

'Head of a croc, front legs and mane of a lion and a hippo's butt. Probably not too fast in a sprint but she's always ready to chomp anyone who reaches judgement in Duat with a guilty conscience.'

*Guilt. Don't start me on that . . .*

Amy shuddered and quickly looked up at the tomb ceilings. They were painted a beautiful blue colour and splatted with stars as fat as yellow starfish. Monstrous or not, all the pictures were fascinating. She could imagine Egyptian painters sweating away as they covered the walls with plaster then tried to keep their hands steady to draw. She loved seeing the faint lines of brush strokes where artists had coloured round the black outlines. It must have been great fun to grind powders to mix paint. She even spotted a brown similar to the pigment on her own limestone picture.

The boys used a muddle of English and Arabic to discuss various gods. She heard scraps of talk about the afterlife as well as the underworld of Duat and various gods – Osiris, Anubis, Ra, Seth . . . too many names to remember! She left them to it and concentrated on the crazy zoo of animals populating each tomb.

She saw crocodiles cruising along rivers on neat reed boats. Dark owls glared out from streams of hieroglyphic writing. Snakes reared up and rasped tongues at bird-headed gods. A grey heron flapped its wings, like a phoenix rising from death. Bees, baboons, rams, rabbits . . . the tombs were crawling with wildlife! There was only one creature she couldn't find.

There was no golden-eyed cat slyly winking.

She checked her phone as soon as she got back out in daylight again. No messages. Just the picture of her sister and Owen.

'Bet you'd take your phone to the afterlife if you were an ancient Egyptian,' Jason taunted.

Amy shoved it back in her bag, squashing any disappointment. 'Except then I wouldn't have a phone.'

'You know what I mean. C'mon, what would you be buried with?'

'I want to be cremated.'

'OK, but just imagine you were planning for the afterlife.'

'I don't believe in life after death.'

'No, neither do I, *exactly*, only if I did, I'd want to be prepared.'

'Ooh, what a boy scout.'

'Explorer Scout, actually,' he said proudly. 'If you must know, I'd make sure I was ready for the afterlife – food, drink, furniture, all that sort of thing. I'd have a copy of the *Book of the Dead* in my coffin, too, like the ancient burials. It's got all the spells you need for defeating demons in the underworld.'

'*Duat for Dummies?*'

Jason laughed. She enjoyed that. Decided to play along.

'OK, Scout Boy, how about stuff to do? You could get seriously bored in eternity.'

'Lots of books, of course. *Lord of the Rings*, anything on military history and *The Count of Monte Cristo*. That'd keep me happy for a couple of centuries.'

'I'd have music.'

'Can't live without your MP3 player?'

'Did they have music in those days? Plinky-plink string instruments?'

'Of course they had music! They even had board games.'

'Oh right, like Monopoly?'

'More like draughts. There's a game called senet – a game of life and death. First player to get all their pieces round the board to the end *dies* and they're the winner.'

'For real?'

'God no – it wouldn't be very popular if there was only a fifty per cent survival rate for players. The Egyptians had loads of games and amusements – gave them something to do instead of sitting round looking at the wall and waiting for TV to be invented.'

'I'm not gonna die if there's no TV! Anyway, you said you'd take books – they're modern, so I can have modern stuff too. Like DVDs. Plus my duvet and pillows.'

'That cuddly toy you can't live without?'

'I don't have any!'

'Not even a plastic pony with a rainbow mane?'

'The one you deliberately dropped in the punch bowl that Christmas years ago? You're *so* dead if you ever mention that again, *and* I'll rob your tomb.'

Amy couldn't resist opening her phone one more time, as Jason stopped to buy some water.

'Who's that?' He pointed to the photo on display.

*Snap.* The happy moment broke.

'Nobody. Just my sister Claire and her boyfriend . . . Owen.'

'Bet they're jealous you're in Egypt.'

Amy erupted. 'Do you have to keep going on about Egypt? I'm sick of the place. Sick of you. Shut up, and, just *shut up!*'

She pushed her way through the crowds looking for solitude, but there was no hiding from the sun's unblinking stare.

# 11 The Lady of the House

*O Shabti which has been made for this person, if this person is detailed for duty or an unpleasant task – to cultivate the fields, to water the riverbank, to fetch and carry – you shall say, 'Here I am!'*

(*Book of the Dead*)

'Is this the boy?'

The lady's voice was as soft and transparent as fine linen gauze. She made no sound as she settled into her chair, though Shabti could still hear the echoes of wings beating. He remembered the heron he'd seen on the roof of the house and wondered if it was nearby.

'This is the one.' Hob stepped from one foot to another, as if he didn't want to contaminate the floor with his dusty reed sandals.

The lady's words all seemed to be coming from far

away. 'He doesn't look dangerous. Not even remotely. And he's very dirty.'

Up to this point Shabti had been awed by the white house. On hearing himself abused so casually something flipped inside him.

'You'd be dirty too!'

'It speaks?'

'Quiet!' Hob barked.

Shabti's lips sealed tight. He lifted his head and glared at Hob, letting his eyes do the talking.

'Rude, too,' the lady murmured.

Just a girl, Shabti thought to himself. Not worth getting angry about. No, not just a girl – a very rich and powerful girl. Regardless of the house and the quiet assumption of authority in her voice, her clothes told that much. She wore a dress of summery green with heavy beading at the hem and round the collar. Her hair had been hennaed to a rich red colour then divided into perfect plaits that looped around her head in a fascinating pattern. Her skin was darker than Shabti's own, but not burnt, just a lovely deep brown, shining with expensive oils and fragrant with equally expensive perfumes. Was that jasmine he sniffed? Hard to tell, the air was so heavy with myrrh and frankincense and a fine dusting of cinnamon. The girl's hands were decorated with delicate henna designs and her eyes outlined with deep black kohl.

It was her eyes that awed him most.

Was there anyone behind them? They were a deep, dark brown but misted slightly. Was she blind? Apparently not. She saw him staring at her and was puzzled. He looked down, focusing on the necklace that hung low on her chest. The chain carried a startling design – an eye so crusted with jewels that it ought to have caught every bit of light and scattered it out again. In fact it was solid and dull, more like a lump of carved stone weighing her down. It shouldn't have drawn his attention so insistently; shouldn't have made his too-busy mind prickle even more than before. There was no hiding from the eye.

'Who are you?' the girl demanded to know. 'Speak!'

It seemed she too had the power to command him against his will.

'My name is Shabti.'

She laughed – a sound like morning birdsong. 'Is that what Hob called you? Of course, you don't have a real name, do you?'

'I do!'

'Oh, you do? Perhaps you would be kind enough to tell me your name, *Shabti*?'

His mouth opened, but no name came out. 'I don't know what my name is.'

'Idiot!' hissed Hob. 'Tell my lady where you've hidden her things.'

'What things?'

'The things you stole, demon boy! Where are they?'

'How *dare* you call me a demon?' he shouted back. 'How *dare* you call me a thief! I haven't stolen anything except enough food to keep me half alive, and that's true, I swear it!'

No command in the world was going to stop him defending his own honour. He wouldn't stand for being so badly humiliated, not in front of this noble lady.

'What about my beaded bracelet?' she said.

'What about it?'

'You stole it!'

'I didn't steal anything!'

'Except food and beer,' Hob interrupted.

Shabti went red. 'That's different. I've got to eat, haven't I?'

The girl stopped playing with a tassel on her cushion. 'Are you hungry, boy?'

'Hungry? I'm so hungry I could eat *you*, not that you'd make more than a mouthful.'

Hob began to uncurl his whip. 'With your permission, my lady . . . ?'

'Wait.' She held up one slender hand. A cascade of golden bracelets shimmered down to her elbow. Shabti wondered how she'd even noticed one bracelet was missing. 'Why is he hungry, Hob?'

'He can't be. He's lying. The workers don't get hungry, or thirsty.'

'Do the workers lie?'

'No, never. At least, not till this one started.'

'I don't tell lies and I'm not a thief,' Shabti interrupted. Then he stopped. How did he know what sort of person he was if he couldn't remember anything beyond a few miserable days?

'What are you then?' asked the lady. 'Do you come from the red land? From Deshret?' Her eyes clouded even as she said the word.

'No! I mean, I don't think so. What's it got to do with you, anyway? I just want to leave here. Go home. Go anywhere else.'

'Home . . .' her voice wafted. 'I don't think you have a home, boy. None of us do. You are in the black land now, in Kemet, working for me. That's how it has always been and always will be. There is nothing but what you see around you and nowhere else to go.'

'If that's what you want to think.'

He didn't care that he was defying her, didn't care that Hob was ready to flay the skin off his back. He was sick of every little thing about this place, Kemet or Deshret, or wherever he was. He deliberately turned away to sulk. He could still hear the argument about him.

Hob was saying, 'He could be from Deshret – they're getting closer every night. Filthy scum! Polluting the river with their foul limbs and keeping the night birds awake with the sound of their weapons.'

'He looks like a boy. A dirty, arrogant boy.'

'With leave, my lady, he's been nothing but trouble since I found him.'

'He's hungry, we can at least see to that. Satipy – some food!'

'And drink,' Shabti muttered.

'Drinks too. Don't stand there gawping at him – go!'

He heard the servant's sandals slap-slapping as she ran in the direction of the kitchen. Before too long Satipy had returned, carrying a tray covered in delicate bowls. Each bowl held a sliver of some delicious fruit.

Hob was disgusted. 'Why feed him when I could thrash him?'

'Leave him with me, Hob. I know you have so many other duties and concerns. Bind his hands, if you must.'

Shabti shovelled as much food into his mouth as he could before Hob took a leather thong and tied his wrists together behind his back.

The overseer leaned in close to his ear and menaced, 'One word of complaint from my lady, one sign of threat from you, and I'll consider it a pleasure to watch Rip and Bite satisfying *their* hunger on your puny little bones, understand?'

When he'd gone, Satipy was ordered forward to trickle sweet wine into Shabti's mouth. It tasted like liquid heaven and made him feel human again. Unfortunately, the long-forgotten luxury made him more ashamed of his shabby clothes, his dirt and open wounds.

'So, boy,' said the lady. 'You say you haven't taken my things and yet Hob believes you may have caused the recent earthquake. He says you've broken the balance here.'

Shabti shook his head. It suddenly ached as if little cracks were spreading out from the back of his skull. Just his imagination.

'I've already told you, I don't know anything. Hey – Ta Miu!' He broke off as the fat fluffball trotted into the room.

The girl frowned. 'How did you know her name?'

'I read her collar.'

'You can read?'

'Looks like it.'

'Why can you read?'

'I don't know! Because somebody taught me, I suppose.'

'Nobody reads except me. At least . . . that's what I thought. I see words all the time, pouring down from the ceiling, splashing on the floor. Words, sounds, sentences, spells, drip, drip, drip . . .'

The lady's hands wafted in the air as if she were swishing them through an invisible cascade. She was so light she seemed almost to be floating above the floor, not treading on it. He was reminded again of the elegant grey heron, aloof on the white house roof.

'What's your name really, boy? Tell me.'

'Shabti. Or I don't know.'

'You don't know. Well. You may as well know that I *do* have a name. I am Lady Anhai.'

That evening was the strangest he'd yet spent in Kemet. First, Lady Anhai ordered Satipy to fetch more perfume to scent the room. Shabti had a quick sniff at his armpits. Yes, perfume would be a good idea. Unfortunately, Satipy returned with her head low and her sandals scuffling the floor.

'A thousand apologies, Mistress, but the perfume has gone.'

'The bottle's empty?'

'No, my lady. The bottle's gone.'

'Are you sure you looked for it properly? It's the blue lotus bottle, with the jasmine scent. You can't have lost that too!'

Satipy kept her eyes low. 'Not lost, Mistress.'

Anhai turned her cloudy eyes on Shabti.

'Have you got my perfume, boy?'

'What, stuffed in my kilt? Hidden in my hair? How could I possibly have your perfume?'

Satipy said slyly, 'Shall I call the overseer, Mistress?'

Anhai wafted her hand. 'No, no, let it go. Nothing to worry about.' She sat in silence for a while, her foot gently bobbing up and down. Shabti was entranced by her fine woven sandals and very conscious of the fact that he was barefoot. That didn't seem right somehow.

Anhai told Shabti to sit up properly – quite difficult to do with bound hands. When he objected she shrugged and said he shouldn't be so argumentative . . . which immediately made him argue. A short, bald servant in a red tunic appeared with rolls of papyrus which were spread out on the floor.

'Read those!' said the delicate autocrat, tapping one foot on the floor.

Shabti tried to resist the order. For a few moments he almost thought he could, then his willpower snapped and he found himself bending to look over the texts.

'Er, this one reads, *There once was a rich mouse who lived in a fine palace attended by many cats. Every day the cats brought perfumed wigs, spiced honey cakes and soft . . .*'

'Stop! Do you know this story?'

Good question. He had to think hard.

'Is it the one about the servants who trick their master into making friends with a snake, only the master is a mouse and the snake is hungry and . . .'

'That's enough.' Anhai's eyes were unusually bright and her voice was sad. 'Satipy reads me stories every night, but only after I tell her what to say. She doesn't know any of her own. Do you know any stories? I've heard nothing but the same ones for . . . for ever, I think.'

'I don't remember any stories,' he said stubbornly, even though there were all sorts of soft-coloured memories tickling the back of his brain now he'd seen papyrus writing again.

'If you don't know any stories, do you play senet? I can tell you the rules.'

'I *know* the rules.'

'Come and play, then.'

'I will – if you untie my hands.'

'You want to *touch* the senet board? You can't, you're dirty.'

'I could get clean.'

'Use my bath? Don't be ridiculous! That's where I wash!'

'So I'll stay dirty. I don't care,' he lied.

'Why should you care? Yes, why do you care about anything? There's something wrong with you, boy. You don't belong here.'

He couldn't help thinking the same thing about her. 'So, do you want to play senet or not?'

'Are you talking to me?'

'No, the cat,' he snapped sarcastically.

King looked up from the rug where he'd settled for an after-dinner snoozle. Shabti felt like he had allies, especially when Ta Miu chose to fuss around his scabby ankles.

'Very well,' Anhai sighed. 'I'll move the pieces for you.'

'Bring me some water and I'll wash my hands at least. I wouldn't want to contaminate your precious game.'

Anhai pretended to ignore him, and the treachery of her cats. She casually summoned Satipy again and ordered water for washing. Satipy's expression seemed to suggest a fleeting, *about time too*. She clearly objected to serving the boy and left quickly, her nose wrinkling.

Water was poured into a beautiful pottery dish decorated with a rich blue glaze and the fine black lines of unfolding lotus flowers. A folded linen towel was set to one side, as well as a small pot of scented oil for soaping. Looking at his hands, cracked with soil in every crease, Shabti reckoned it would more likely take a few bucketfuls to get them even vaguely presentable. A new memory jostled – of servants kneeling to wash his hands for him and patting them gently dry before rubbing the skin with silky creams.

'Hurry up,' said Anhai.

He didn't answer. He suddenly thought he saw something in the water. Was it a pattern on the bottom of the dish? It looked like it was moving, swirling, coiling, rising . . .

With a shout of disgust he pushed the bowl away, spilling water across the floor. He'd definitely seen some kind of creature lurking in there, crocodile-like, but with wild hair.

When Satipy righted the bowl again it was innocently empty.

'Sorry,' he mumbled. 'I slipped.'

'Idiot,' said Anhai. 'I'm bored of you now. Satipy, call Hob. Tell him to bring the boy again tomorrow, and make sure his hands are clean before he returns.'

Shabti smarted under the abrupt dismissal and he sulked all the way back to the compound, where he was forced to stay until the lady of the white house summoned him once more.

# 12 Top of the World

*There is always something moving, something doing . . .*
(Amelia B. Edwards, *A Thousand Miles Up the Nile*)

Early start?!

Getting up at *five o'god* in the morning wasn't just early, it was more like hardly going to bed!

Amy was halfway across the Nile before she noticed her black jumper was on back to front. She swizzled it round. They weren't alone on the river. Small boats motored up and down, and an exodus of floating hotels were slowly heading upstream, like a herd of prehistoric beasts in search of warmer pastures. Dawn was chilly and a haunting mist covered the river and the fields of the west bank. She was glad of her jumper, even if it was getting pretty shapeless and sullied.

'Are you awake yet?' Jason asked. 'You don't quite look

human.' He was wearing a snug fleece with a surprisingly trendy logo. His socks matched and his eyes weren't crusty with sleep.

'This better be good,' she muttered, but she wasn't really cross. By then, her fourth day in Egypt, she felt slightly less like a stranger in an alien landscape. She was familiar with the shape of the dark desert cliffs, the silhouettes of palm trees and the haunting call to prayer. Somewhere in those cliffs was the Windy Wadi and a door down into darkness.

The *Action Archaeology!* team had spent two days clearing a safe entrance to the new site TT440 – now called the Cat Tomb. Amy and Jason had been left to amuse themselves touring the temples of Luxor and Karnak, and cruising through the colourful downtown *souk*. In the evening Amy had hovered at the edge of the group discussing the day's work round a riverside table of food and beer. Objects blocking the doorway to the tomb had been removed from the site. Some were even brought out on show, when the hotel waiters were nowhere near. In addition to the perfume jar and lamp, found on that first exciting evening, there were some rough cooking pots, a stack of reed baskets, and, most precious of all, an exquisite bead bracelet. The red and blue beads alternated with tiny carved charms.

116

'Like it?' Amy's dad asked.

She loved it. 'Will they put it in the Cairo Museum?'

Ellie Powell looked up at that. 'It's pretty, but the bods at Cairo won't think it's anything special next to the flashy wonders salvaged from royal tombs. It'll probably get a number and go in a drawer somewhere. It's a shame. The museum I'll be working at, in Harrofield, they'd love to have something like it on show. It's gorgeous.'

Amy's dad was feeling generous. 'Who knows, now we've found an intact burial, I might just be able to wangle a loan from the authorities. Some little bits and bobs for Yorkshire local yokels to enjoy.'

'Oh, give over with your Yorkshire jokes!' Ellie groaned. 'I was a little eight-year-old yokel myself once. I went to an Egyptian exhibition at Harrofield Museum and saw a mask of Anubis and a mummified frog. That's when I knew I wanted to be an archaeologist. Even better, as soon as this dig's finished I'm starting a job there as assistant curator!'

Clayton just said, 'Bless!'

Well, there they were now, having adventures in the Cat Tomb while Amy was . . . Amy had no idea where she was going, except that she was heading to the west bank with a small group of tourists and Jason Henderson. The noise of the motorboat engine easily drowned their yawns. Then Jason said, 'Look,' so everyone twisted round in their seats and did just that.

It was the most beautiful sight. Eight or ten coloured balloons hung in the mist above the Theban cliffs. Not party balloons – vast hot-air balloons, slowly drifting along the edge of the desert.

'You can't come to Luxor and not take a balloon ride over the Valley of the Kings,' said Jason. 'Hey! That even made you smile.'

The smile switched off, but Amy couldn't squash the sense of excitement inside. It made her tummy wriggle.

*Wait till I tell Claire!*

She flipped her phone lid open, just as the boat bumped to a halt at the far bank. Flipped it shut. No messages.

'*Yalla!*' called the Egyptian boy who'd been steering. He revved up the engine so a fug of black smoke followed them over the wobbly gangplank to dry land.

Amy turned to Jason, who was loving all the activity. 'You planned this?'

'It was your dad's idea.'

*Dad?* That was about as believable as the world being flat or Elvis spotted alive and well and stacking supermarket shelves. Dad wouldn't be caught dead doing touristy things.

A bus collected them from the riverbank and

eventually trundled to a halt on one of the tracks that cut through the patchwork of fertile fields bordering the river, to where a red and white balloon was being coaxed into life by a noisy air fan. A group of lads in football shirts and dirty trainers organized everything with easy-going efficiency. Amy spotted Mazen among them, still tripping over the hem of his galabeya. There was no sign of the dog Anubis. Mazen saw her and waved. She couldn't help waving back.

Soon the balloon was fully inflated and raring to go. Amy hesitated. 'Don't we have to do a risk assessment – all that health and safety stuff?'

Jason laughed. 'It's Egypt! You get in and enjoy the ride. Lighten up – and hold on tight!'

'*Yalla!*' Mazen called. 'Let's go!'

Her jumper got snagged on the wickerwork basket as she clambered in. The balloon was massive overhead. She panicked. The basket was lined with soft, red cotton velvet, but it only reached to her chest and there were no safety harnesses or restraints.

'Ready?'

More people were squashing into the basket, so Jason moved in closer, using some of his height to shield her from the sudden intense heat as flames ate up the oxygen under the balloon opening.

'Everybody is OK?' Mazen called from the road.

Another blast of heat made all the passengers flinch. 'I think I'm getting out . . .' Amy began, then stopped. Where was the ground going? Why was Mazen getting smaller? 'Are we . . .? Ohmygod, we're going up and I never noticed. Everything's so . . . smooth. Easy. Just gliding . . . Wow!'

As the sky spread out and the ground dropped away a flock of cameras appeared, bobbing and clicking from every angle. Again and again flames burst upwards. It wasn't cold at all. On the contrary, Amy was baking in her big black sweater.

'Take it off, I'll hold it for you,' Jason offered.

'No!' Her cheeks reddened, not from heat. 'I'm fine.'

Fine? She felt more than fine! She felt absolutely marvellous, as if she'd abandoned something heavy on the ground and that was why the balloon rose so swiftly and smoothly. Her heart was as light as the air all around.

Egypt spread out beneath them. To the east, the misty river, edged by buildings and green fields. From the air she could see how sudden the dividing line was between fields and desert. Just a couple of paces would take you from green to red – life to death. She imagined she was floating above the centuries. It was easy to wash out evidence of modern life to see the landscape as it would have been in ancient times – the same fields, the same dusty houses filled with the same sorts of people.

Westward, where the desert began, was the threshold of death in ancient times. Life dwindled there. Miles and miles and miles . . . She'd never seen anywhere so featureless, so uninhabited. You could set off walking and go on . . . for ever, it seemed. No food, no water, no shelter. It wasn't surprising the ancient Egyptians had feared the red land.

'The desert is Seth's terrain,' Jason said. 'He's the traditional bad-guy god. Lord of Chaos, enemy of Ra and Osiris and all that. The myths say he tore Osiris up and scattered the pieces everywhere. Osiris's wife Isis found all of them except one crucial bit that had been swallowed by a catfish.'

'Crucial for what?'

'Don't ask, honey,' interrupted an American woman who'd been listening in.

'Isis kind of managed without it,' Jason continued, with a touch of embarrassment. 'She gave birth to a son called Horus, who went off to battle Seth.'

'And tore him to pieces?'

'Not permanently. That's the thing about Egyptian mythology. Chaos is never completely wiped out. Seth is there to balance the forces of order – you can't have one without the other. Balance is pretty crucial. It's the eternal battle of good and evil. What matters is which side you choose.'

'The Dark Side every time,' said Amy promptly.

'I can see you in a Darth Vader helmet.'

'Ha ha ha.'

'Excuse me,' said the American lady, tugging on Jason's arm. 'Aren't you that boy from the TV show, what's it called? *Archaeology in Action*, am I right? It is you, isn't it? Julian Harrison?'

'Er, Jason Henderson, yes.'

Trapped three thousand feet in the air, he couldn't escape from the sudden demand for autographs even if he'd wanted to.

Amy was forced right into the corner of the basket. She winced as her ribs bruised – an unwelcome reminder that she wasn't completely healed yet. No need to think about that now. She let fresh, cool air blow away any bad feelings, thinking, *Might as well enjoy the view before we crash.* Her streaky black and red hair wafted away from her face. She was drinking in the whole experience.

They floated on . . . above houses scattered among the dry desert foothills around the Theban tombs . . . past the temple of female Pharaoh Hatshepsut, a place so vast it even dwarfed the massive coach park built before it . . .

then over folds in the desert plateau that hid secrets archaeologists still ached to discover.

The night before, there'd been a big discussion about security at the Cat Tomb. Farouk's integrity was never in doubt, even though the locals, historically, had a dreadful reputation for pilfering from ancient sites, encouraged by the greed of both amateur and professional collectors. The dog Anubis had been put on guard to stop any enterprising souvenir seekers. Farouk's men would deter the hardcore treasure-hunters.

'Little beggars flog everything on the internet,' Ellie ranted. 'All artefacts belong in a museum.'

'Don't they belong exactly where they are?' Amy had ventured. 'As soon as you start digging somewhere on a site you wreck the place and it never looks the same again.'

She was amazed to see Ellie nodding agreement. 'Absolutely . . . in a perfect world. Excavation is destructive by its very nature. It's why we record everything we do so meticulously. Well, usually. The trouble is, tomb robbers have plagued this area almost since burials began. In some parts of the country archaeologists work on site by day and thieves clear it at night, then . . .'

'. . . the little beggars flog it on the internet.'

'Right.'

Amy's dad leaned into the argument. 'Never forget, both of you, that if it wasn't for archaeologists we wouldn't know as much as we do about life in the past. Besides,' he paused to grin, 'it makes great TV.'

TV was Jason's downfall. He was pestered for the rest of the balloon flight. Amy thought he handled the attention pretty well. She'd seen him on a couple of *Action Archaeology!* episodes and knew he belonged in front of a camera.

*What about me?* she wondered, as she leaned over the edge of the balloon basket. *Where do I belong?*

When she pulled out her fragment of limestone, the cat's paw was, not surprisingly, pointing straight at the ground. Somewhere below was the Cat Tomb.

Slowly, slowly, the balloon began to drift down. The operator kept up a cheerful patter, assuring them the approaching power lines weren't nearly as close as they looked, and that there wasn't the slightest chance of them landing on the rooftops of the village just underneath. Lower and lower they went. Amy held on to every last second. The balloon basket scraped on dried stalks of sugarcane stumps. Touchdown. No, they rose again, as if flapped into flight by the agitated gestures of a farmer with a face the colour of old tobacco. As they skimmed clods of soil, the bus-load of lads appeared to whisk the basket to firmer ground. Without any fuss, they eased the collapsing silken sac on to a vast tarpaulin, letting sunlight pour into the basket.

Amy was still grinning as she hoisted herself over the basket edge and on to the ground. Her fingers tingled where Jason grabbed her hand as he climbed out.

'*Yalla, yalla!*' There was Mazen, clapping dementedly. He pulled at Amy's jumper, unravelled a few more stitches. 'This bus, this way,' he said. '*Yalla!*'

Where were they going now? More surprises?

'Breakfast,' said Jason. The minibus slewed up clouds of dust as it stopped outside a jumble of mud bricks and corrugated metal sheets, topped with a gaudy awning. 'Not just breakfast, the *best* breakfast in Egypt. This café is my third favourite place in the world.'

Amy found herself hustled on to a wooden bench and faced with a thimble-sized cup of liquid grit.

'Wakey wakey!' Mazen grinned. He downed his cup of strong coffee in a few quick swallows and went to join a group of boys loitering about at the far end of the café. Their Arabic was so fast and slangy Jason gave up trying to understand. He was far from fluent.

White plates appeared on the table. Amy stared at the warm bread envelopes that were stuffed with fat, fluffy yellow omelettes. Rounds of soft cheese were just waiting to be tasted. Rosy red tomato slices were sprinkled with bright green curls of parsley. For the first time in a long while she actually felt hungry. That novel sensation lasted all of ten minutes. After that the plates were empty.

'Are we stuck here?' she asked quickly, before any burps could come.

'Mazen says the bus has gone back to the river. We've got guests at the wadi today.'

'The X-ray lady from Cairo?'

'Yeah, the radiographer. Well, actually, she's an Egyptologist with a seriously good reputation. Ellie knows her from going to a course of lectures in Cairo. Sounds like they got on pretty well. Hey, you want seconds?'

There was a pause and an unconvincing, 'No.'

More minutes passed; more food was eaten. A bus horn broke the idyll. There was Ellie Powell, hanging out of the window yelling, '*Yalla! Yalla!*'

Mazen shooed his charges on to the bus then went to sit up front with the driver.

'Another brother,' Jason murmured.

'I can guess just by looking at you the balloon trip was good!' Ellie exclaimed. 'Tell me all about it in a mo, only first I want you to meet my friend, the one and only Dr

Rosa Hassan. This is her glamorous assistant, Dan . . .'

Dan didn't look up from his comic book.

'. . . and that there is at least ten tons of equipment that all needs lugging the length of the wadi to the Chariot Tomb. Today's the day we find out who's inside the sarcophagus!'

Amy was surprised to see that Dr Hassan was a young woman, probably in her twenties still. She had long black hair, glossed into a high ponytail, and stylish specs.

Ellie was in top spirits. 'You'll never guess what Rosa's brought!'

Jason glanced at the piles of silver cases. 'The X-ray kit, obviously.'

'Well, yeah, but better than that.'

'CAT scan equipment.'

'Better.'

'A magic wand that can bring the dead to life and make them tell their own history?'

'Oh, stop being so dull! Look!' Ellie produced a small cardboard box with a flourish. 'Isn't it lovely? Couldn't you just kiss the woman? She fetched it all the way from a western supermarket in Cairo, just for me!'

Rosa Hassan's reward for such an errand was obvious: Ellie couldn't be more delighted. She was holding an unopened box of virgin tea bags. Genuine Yorkshire Tea.

Amy turned away. Cups of tea made her think of Mum and Claire, at home in the kitchen, nattering and bickering comfortably. Time to check her phone again. No messages. Why would there be? They obviously didn't want to be in touch and that was that. She felt cold despite the hot coffee and morning sun.

Jason looked over her shoulder. 'I'm surprised you're getting messages through. The signal's non-existent on the west bank, and the local mast in Luxor is switched off for repairs. No one else's mobile works.'

Ah. No mast. No signal. Hence no messages . . . Suddenly the sun seemed warmer.

# 13 Missing Pieces

*It seems almost desecration to trouble that long peace
and break that eternal silence.*

(Howard Carter, *The Discovery of the
Tomb of Tutankhamun*)

The next time Shabti was summoned to see Lady Anhai, he was allowed to wash his hands and face first, using a shallow clay dish filled with brackish water. No amount of scrubbing could wipe away the dark rings under his eyes, or the yellow tinge on his skin. Hob had taken to tossing him scraps of food, as if he were a whining dog. Stale bread and pulpy fruit were better than nothing, but not what he wanted.

*Not what I'm used to.*

This was the phrase buzzing in his mind like a trapped wasp. He only had to look over to the white house to feel twisty inside; only had to see the grey heron sunning itself to be hot with resentment.

Having Ta Miu welcome him with a loud purr was calming at least. She kept him company as he waited in the cool room for Lady Anhai to appear. The cat's fur was soft as she wove herself round and round his legs. He almost forgot the ache in his bones and the irritation of his many blisters and scabs. Just as one wound healed, he'd stumble in the fields and open up a new one.

Hob supervised his work personally now, to make sure he never slackened or tried to run away. If Hob's duties called him away to another part of the compound he only had to shout, 'Shabti, where are you?' and Shabti had no choice but to call out, 'Here I am!' in reply. If Shabti ever lifted his head to look across to the green sward of the riverbank, Rip and Bite would instantly leap up and growl.

Even so, he hadn't given up hope of escaping. Ta Miu's fur reminded him of the rope he could spin to lower himself down into the secret underground room. He gave her a quick grooming, coming away with a handful of soft stuff, which he tucked into his kilt. The fur and his hoe were all he owned in the world.

Unlike Lady Anhai. Living in her lovely house, with servants and a shady garden, she seemed to have the perfect life. He couldn't understand why thinking of her made him so uneasy. Even though he was the stranger in this land, Anhai didn't seem to belong either. Particularly the second time he saw her, he was struck by how she seemed to drift rather than exist. She didn't seem quite as vivid as before, like someone walking backwards into a mist.

On this second visit to the white house Satipy presented him with a plate of honey cakes, each as light as a feather and delicately flavoured with powdery cinnamon. He ate five, quickly. They dissolved on his tongue and didn't stop his stomach trying to shrink in on itself. Ta Miu was presented with a beautiful glazed dish containing strips of roast duck. She purred as she ate, then took herself off to a corner to cough up a hairball.

Lady Anhai appeared and settled in her chair so lightly, so silently, Shabti wasn't aware she was in the room until he heard her sandals tap on the floor. She still wore the dull eye necklace around her neck. It still drew his gaze and made him anxious and eager at the same time. In dreams he'd often felt the weight of a red eye pressing him down, squeezing his breath out century by century . . . At the same time he'd be reaching out as if the eye could offer some sort of elusive salvation.

Anhai sneered at him. 'So you haven't run off to

Deshret then, little spy? Back to your den in the red land?'

'That's not where I'm from. And, hello to you too.'

'You haven't learned any manners either. Why should you? My servants don't learn things, they just do them.' She tipped her head on one side, like an inquisitive bird. 'Is there something you wish to tell me? Some secrets to unburden?'

He coloured, thinking of the invisible hole, even though he knew she was coaxing him to confess to thefts he hadn't committed.

'No. Nothing. Except I'm ready to challenge you to a game of senet, if you dare.'

Anhai clapped her hands for Satipy to fetch the senet board.

'I haven't played for . . . for . . . since . . .' Her voice slowly vanished. 'I mean, I'd like to play now. I'll be frogs, you be hedgehogs.'

'I don't want to be hedgehogs.'

'Hedgehogs always go first.'

'But they start further back on the board . . .'

'Only on the first throw!'

'I want to be frogs!'

'*I want, I want,*' she mimicked. 'What does it matter what *you* want? Kemet is *my* place and it's all about

132

what *I* want, in case you hadn't noticed.'

'I hardly need to notice when you oh-so-politely ram the fact down my throat every time you pucker open your mouth to whinge.'

Anhai's mouth dropped open. 'How dare you! I want you out of my sight.'

'I want, I want,' he echoed back at her. 'You've got everything you want, thanks to all *my* hard work. Oh, don't look like that. Haven't you ever been teased before?'

'Who would possibly tease *me*? My servants? Ridiculous!'

Shabti watched Satipy carry the senet board over to her mistress, then looked over at the silent paunchy man who always hovered nearby. No sign of teasing from them.

'Not your servants. Maybe your . . . your . . .' He squeezed his eyes tight-closed in the effort to conjure up a word. 'Family! That's it! Maybe your *family* tease you. Brothers. Sisters.' He opened his eyes and breathed out with release. For a moment the two children just stared at each other.

Neither of them had more than the faintest of faint idea what a family was; what 'brother' or 'sister' meant.

Anhai turned away first. 'I don't want to play senet any more. Go away.'

Stung, he untangled his legs and stood up. 'I'd only have beaten you anyway. Easily.'

Although she had been drifting away into a vague assumption of proud indifference, now Anhai was pulled back. Shabti was pleased, though he couldn't quite understand why. Because she was actually talking to him? Because she suddenly seemed less wispy than usual?

Satipy jumped at the sound of snapping fingers. She began to set the pieces out again, subtly indicating that her mistress should be frogs.

Suddenly Shabti didn't care if he had frogs, hedgehogs or minuscule tadpoles. He glanced up at the windows facing the garden. Perhaps tonight would be a good night to make a better investigation of the invisible hole. He could take a few supplies, spin new thread, lower himself down . . .

'Forgive me, Mistress.' Satipy's voice quavered. Her long fingers trembled as she emptied the little wooden tray slotted inside the senet board, then searched around the stool. 'I can't . . . can't find all the pieces.'

Anhai sighed so deeply the room seemed to shimmer.

'How many pieces are gone?'

'Two, Mistress. One frog, one hedgehog.'

'Then we'll play with only four pieces each, not five. Add the missing pieces to the list.'

'Yes, Mistress.'

'It's not the same without all the pieces,' Shabti complained.

'Well, read to me instead. Satipy – a cushion for the boy, just an old one, he's still filthy. He can finish the story of the master mouse and the tricky cat servants . . .'

'No!' he snapped. 'Something's gone missing and you just want me to sit on a fat cushion and read to you as if nothing's happened? Don't you want to know where the senet pieces have gone? Who's taken them? Who's taking all the things from your house and the compound? Doesn't it bother you that strange things are happening round here? Doesn't *anything* worry you at all?'

Anhai's thoughts seemed to be floating far away. 'Worry? I never worry. Why do you? It makes you frown, then your skin crumples up.'

'Who cares about that? It's just skin.'

'Care? I don't care. Not about anything. This, all this, it's perfect. Wonderful. Everything I could possibly want.' She turned in a slow circle, letting her arms drift like weak wings.

'Are you drugged? Do they put something in the tea – poppy juice or something? You're dreamy all the time, like nothing matters.'

'Nothing does. Here, puss, come here, Ta Miu.'

She bent to the cat, but Ta Miu had found something under the chair and was patting it tentatively to see if it would make good sport. Shabti darted forward and picked the object up. It was a small gaming piece, carved in the shape of a tiny hedgehog.

'From your senet game,' he said.

'You see! Nothing's missing after all! So just sit down and tell me a story.'

'I can't remember any right now.'

'That's no use to me.'

'I didn't come here to be useful to you!'

'What are you for, then?'

'I don't know!' he shouted. 'But at least I want to find out!'

He was only stopped from storming out of the house by a sudden throb from the sore spot on the back of his skull. He grabbed his head and swallowed the pain down. The wasp near his ear buzzed louder than ever before.

'Are you all right? You look awful.'

'Thank you, my lady. That's about how I feel.'

'Your limp is worse today.'

So she did notice things. 'Just a bit achy.'

It was actually bothering him more than usual, the

deep pain in his left hip. He thought he must have jarred it when running after the white hippo, on his very first day in Kemet. Or perhaps it had been before then, from one of the jagged shards of memory left in his brain.

'Let Satipy bring you something if you're hurt.'

It was hard to speak through the haze. 'Don't – need – anything.'

His vision blurred. He had an image of Anhai hovering over him, wafting him with the faint breeze of feathers. He caught the scent of jasmine perfume and then, when his eyes focused once more, he found he was looking straight at the stool where the senet board was – no, where the senet board *had been*.

Though no one was nearby, somehow it was gone, leaving only a soft dent in the cushion.

This time there would be no reprieve. Almost as the last chimes of Anhai's bell died away, Hob was on the spot, waiting for her instructions.

'Take this conjurer! This thief!' she said. 'Take him far away from the house. Take him to the very edge of the fields, to the river even. Fling him into Deshret if you have to, just make sure I never set eyes on him in the black land again.'

'You're crazy!' Shabti called out, as Hob dragged him none too gently out of her room. 'Something terrible's happening and you're pretending everything's fine. Well it isn't, and it won't be, unless you wake up and do something about it! That's just your problem – you won't do anything!'

Leaving the garden, his heart was as sore as his various physical wounds. How would he be able to sneak all the way through the fields back to the mysterious hole now? How was he going to escape when everything seemed to be conspiring against him?

Or maybe not everything.

Instead of uncoiling his whip and looming over the boy, Hob merely dragged him out into the dust of the compound then shoved him into a quiet corner. Shabti waited for a fist pummelling . . . that never came. Hob looked as menacing as ever – more so with the dying sun turning his muscles a blood-red colour – yet the twist on his face was less of a threat and more of a frown, as if Hob were struggling to make up his mind about something.

Clearly he did, eventually. He looked around the compound then spat in the dirt.

'I don't like you, boy.'

No surprises there, Shabti thought.

'Don't like you, don't hardly trust you. But . . . you're right. Wrong things are happening in Kemet. The earthquake. The missing things.' Hob leaned in closer. His breath was sour with barley beer. 'It was all balanced before, good on one side and bad on the other. Now the balance is upset. Deshret is coming, boy. Deshret and all the monsters in it. If they cross the river then all this is over – this farm, this house, *ruined*. I won't let that happen. *Can't* let that happen.'

'Can they even get across the river?' Shabti asked, tagging a quick, 'Master Hob' on to the end of his question.

'Can they get across? Ay, that's something you and I both would like to know for sure. Only one way to find out. Someone'll have to guard it, now won't they? Some little beggar who's no good for anything else. Yeah, then if that little beggar gets eaten we'll know whether the monsters can cross or not, won't we, now? *Won't we, boy?*'

# 14 Lifting the Coffin Lid

*I could not pass without putting my face in contact
with some decayed Egyptian.*
(Belzoni, excavating at Gourna in the early nineteenth
century)

'You know what?' Ellie said. 'I think we've got this
place all wrong. It's not a tomb. It's a ruddy ancient
Egyptian sauna!'

She finished up another bottle of mineral water and
wiped drops of sweat from her face, using the bottom of
a T-shirt that Amy had coveted the moment she saw the
slogan on it: *What Are You Looking At??!*

On that hot December morning, Amy, Ellie and
the X-ray lady were looking at the sarcophagus in the
Chariot Tomb.

Dr Rosa Hassan raised one well-plucked eyebrow.

'How very inconsiderate of the tomb builders. They designed a room to keep a corpse and grave goods safe for all eternity but were too narrow-minded to plan for future visits from TV crews, not to mention a small lab's worth of equipment.'

'Selfish swine,' Ellie agreed.

Amy looked around the tiny burial chamber that had so far failed to keep either its owner or the grave goods safe. What an awful place the Chariot Tomb was! The bright spotlights only made the dirt of TT439 look darker. Dr Hassan's metal cases and machines contrasted with the worn stone of the sarcophagus, which dominated the space and left them all squashed and sweating.

Kev the cameraman had grumpily moved his equipment from TT440, the Cat Tomb. 'Far more exciting stuff in the other tomb with Tony,' he complained.

He wilted when Rosa's cool brown gaze settled on him.

'As far as I am aware, no body has yet been found in the Cat Tomb,' she said calmly, 'and that is precisely what *we* are here to study. I assume Dr Clayton wants me to continue without him?'

'He'll do a voice-over when they edit the footage,' Ellie said. 'Nothing will drag him out of his new treasure trove.'

'Very well. We'll begin. *If* you've no objections, Kevin?'

Kev shook his head mutely.

Amy had objections. Tons of them! First of all, she hadn't exactly *meant* to say yes when Ellie asked if they wanted to join the X-ray team in the Chariot Tomb. The excitement of the balloon ride had somehow carried her along into the wadi, down the tunnel and into the tomb. Now this enthusiasm was rapidly seeping out of her.

Next, it wasn't fair there was so much secrecy about the Cat Tomb, when she was aching to look inside. Apparently it was OK for Jason to be invited in for his turn in the spotlight, but not the person who'd actually found the tomb in the first place.

Finally, most crucially, the dead body. She didn't want to have anything to do with it.

Tough. Midday found her stuck in the dull tomb with a bunch of technical types and a mummified Egyptian.

She was unwanted, as usual. Rosa quietly recorded preliminary notes, Ellie adjusted lights, Kev was wielding the camera, Dan the technician rigged up a laptop link with the X-ray machine. He never once pulled out his music earphones. As he worked he hummed along to his music – some sort of hysterical dance frenzy as far as Amy could make out. All four wore white coats and face masks, as much to protect themselves as the mummy they were about to investigate.

Amy edged forward to get a closer look at things – and was promptly flattened against the wall of the tiny chamber as Farouk led a group of men inside to lift the heavy stone lid off the sarcophagus.

Rosa bent over the lid just before it was hoisted clear. She traced the red granite images with her gloved finger, in particular the stylized eye.

'How ironic to see the carving of the *wedjat* eye broken. The Eye of Horus is meant to keep things whole.'

'There's nothing whole about this place,' Ellie muttered.

There was a sound of grating rock as the lid was lifted. Amy squeezed her eyes shut. This was too much like grave robbing and body-snatching! She had visions of Dr Frankenstein digging up corpses to make his monster . . . Or exhumations of rotting remains in the crime shows Claire was so addicted to.

*I won't look inside*, she thought. *Definitely won't look at the body.*

Once the lid had been carried out to the antechamber and stored safely, Amy opened her eyes and kept her gaze low. She didn't look anywhere near the sarcophagus. Unfortunately, Kev's camera was also linked to a laptop – the one on a box right at her side. She clamped a hand over her mouth to swallow a sudden scream. A dead face was there on the computer screen, looking right at her, eyes open and alive.

'Fascinating,' said Rosa, through her mask. 'The eyes are visible. Not the originally human eyeballs, of course. These are almond-shaped ceramic eyes, white and black, to mimic an unblinking gaze.'

Amy let out her breath slowly. Of course thousands-year-old eyes couldn't still see! It was stupid to be frightened. Stupid stupid stupid. She found she was shaking. Even if she closed her eyes, she still felt a dead gaze boring into her mind, bringing back memories of another man's eyes locked open, unseeing as rain fell on a white face . . .

Rosa's elegant Egyptian accent penetrated her panicked mind. The scientist continued her calm appraisal while Kev filmed for *Action Archaeology!*

'As you see, the wooden coffins we would have expected to find inside this stone casing are absent. Stolen, possibly even burned. The mummy itself is in plain view. Originally the whole body would have been properly bandaged, each finger, each limb, every part expertly wrapped in strips of linen. Now look, we can see the cloth is stained a nasty brown colour. We assume it has been shredded by robbers in their haste to strip the body of all valuables. The outer shroud, here, is rotted away. The outer binding strips are damaged and disordered. These linen strips are between a hundred millimetres and a hundred and sixty millimetres wide, originally wrapping from the feet upwards to the shoulders. The fine threads and dense weave suggest expensive fabric.'

She took up a magnifying glass. Kev enhanced the focus on his camera.

'There are fragments of what is possibly plant material around the chest area. Maybe a funeral garland.'

Kev pressed *pause* and moved the camera to a different angle.

'Nice that people left flowers,' he said. 'Are those little dried-up buds on the dead bloke's face?'

Rosa produced a thin smile. 'Buds? Do you mean flowers waiting to open? No. Continue recording, if you please. These, within the wrappings, these are dried insects. Possibly the carrion beetle *dermestes*. Ms Clayton, if you please, one of those plastic jars.'

Amy froze like a rabbit in headlights. 'Me?' she mouthed.

'Yes, please.'

No question of refusing, with Kev filming everything for posterity. Amy found a small jar in Rosa's equipment tray, unscrewed the lid and held it out.

'Closer, please.'

Rosa took a set of tweezers from her lab coat pocket and gently lifted three insects from the body and placed them in the jar. Amy could still see their shrivelled bodies through the transparent plastic. Because her fingers trembled, so did the dried beetles.

Rosa spoke to the camera, though her eyes were focused on the human remains before her. 'As the body was processed for death, the beetles will have laid their eggs in the flesh. Then the body was bandaged and buried. The larvae will have hatched and died trying to chew their way out. Fascinating.'

Kev had a very peculiar look on his face as Amy screwed the lid tightly on to the plastic jar. She knew exactly how he felt. How awful, to be buried safely, with hungry little beetles already waiting in your flesh to devour you. She wished she could block out Rosa's commentary, or at least squeal and pretend to faint, like Charlotte Pratt always did during biology dissections at school.

Rosa continued, as if on automatic.

'The skin on the face, where revealed, is brown and leathery and saturated with resin. The resin is solidified in places, but it is apparent that the head wrappings have suffered from damp in the past, causing some resin to dissolve. The general environment of the tomb is very wet. There have been periodic saturations of moisture in the air and evidence of inundations filtering through fissures in the surrounding rock. Intermittent humid periods have severely affected the tomb contents and obviously the mummy itself. To summarize: flood water has caused rotting.

'The eyes have lost their original shape and sunk into the skull, replaced with these two ceramic pieces which I will leave in place for now. Both eyebrows are well preserved and neatly groomed. Most of the soft tissue of the nose has disintegrated. We'll see if the internal bone structures are intact when we X-ray. The right ear has been exposed and is partially decayed.'

'There's a hole in his ear!' Amy blurted out.

Rosa didn't seem to mind. 'Ellie, could you direct the light on the right earlobe. Yes, that is clear. It is a hole pierced for earrings.'

Amy's hand jumped to her own ear, where a cluster of plastic cherries and skulls dangled. Suddenly that one tiny connection made her shiver with the realization that the shape in the coffin had definitely been a person once. What sort of person? What was his name? Could science tell any of this after so many centuries?

They had a quick break – a very necessary chance to gulp down lots of tepid water and wipe away perspiration. Kev rubbed the shoulder that had been holding the camera.

'Creeps me out,' he said. 'I mean, this bloke looks raddled enough, but I keep expecting him to sit up and groan.'

'Too many movies,' laughed Ellie.

Rosa said, 'A mummy is just an ancient cadaver whose soft tissues have partially or wholly resisted decay.'

'But it was human once,' Amy objected. 'I mean, how'd you like it if one day someone dug you up and took pictures of your corpse?'

The scientist's mouth twisted into a wry smile. 'I will be cremated. Unlike this gentleman here . . .' she gestured to the mummy, 'I have no plans to be resurrected into an afterlife, so I won't be needing a physical body.'

'They don't actually live in the corpse when they're dead, though, do they? I mean . . .'

Rosa smiled. 'I understand you. It's not the actual body that is required. This mummy only represents the body used in the afterlife. It is meant to be preserved so that the *ba* spirit – separated at death – can recognize its physical home and find its way back to be whole again. A vital reunion.'

Amy had a sudden vision of a disgruntled *ba* flapping around their heads trying to get back to the body they were poking and prodding for TV. No. That was too fanciful. The tomb was too desolate – long since abandoned by its ghostly soul.

'Now, back to work,' said Rosa. 'I'll take some samples if you, Amy, will hold more dishes for me. Analysis of the hard resin on the mummy will show what plant it came from. If it is something exotic, such as pistachio or cedar resin, this will suggest an elite burial, and we think this is a rich man, yes?'

'Not much use to him now,' Ellie said, looking round the desolate tomb. 'Let's hope he's having more fun in the afterlife, whoever he is.'

'He's a very short man,' Amy said suddenly.

Ellie flourished her tape measure. 'Thigh bones are forty-three point two centimetres on the left and forty four point nine on the right. That puts our Egyptian at . . . oh God, I hate mental maths! Hang on . . . about a hundred and sixty centimetres tall. Say, five foot three inches, give or take. You're right. He's not a big fella.'

They were not done with insects. A large section of the scalp was showing, where linen coverings had rotted or ripped. Partway through an examination of the mummy's remaining hair, Rosa gave a little cry and bent low. Amy saw an image being relayed on to the laptop at her side.

What was that tiny thing, stuck on a shaft of hair?

She had a sudden uncomfortable memory of coming home from infant school with an itchy head. Mum had attacked her with a nit comb and foul-smelling foam that was supposed to be 'apple scented'. Yeah right.

Rosa showed another ghost of a smile, plucked at the hair with her tweezers and held it aloft. 'This, my friends, looks like an ancient Egyptian louse case. I believe you would say, the mummy had nits. Unfortunately it was a common problem in ancient times – even the pharaohs suffered from them.'

Amy had to resist the temptation to scratch her own head in sympathy.

'And that's not all!' Rosa's eyes brightened. 'Look here. This is rather unexpected on a corpse, wouldn't you say? How wonderful that it is the little things which truly come to haunt us across the gulf of time.'

There, nestling in the linen folds around the mummy's neck, was another insect. Not a carrion beetle, or a nit. A mummified wasp.

Even Kev couldn't help but be fascinated as Rosa removed the wasp from the body.

She said, 'If we suppose that the plant material around the mummy's chest is the remains of a flower garland placed by mourners at the funeral, I'd say this little creature was attracted by the scent of the flowers. It flew down to the petals, landed for a moment . . . and was trapped for ever as the coffin lid came down. Perfectly preserved, just like the human host. We cannot travel back across the ages to find something as fleeting as a wasp, but here is one preserved for us, brought forward in time, you might say. This, ladies and gentlemen, is as rare, as precious as a fly in, how do you say . . . ? Amber?'

'Imagine being bugged by the buzz of a wasp for all eternity,' Ellie marvelled, as soon as the camera went off.

More water was needed. They decided to leave the stuffy tomb for a while and take a break in the sunshine. Mazen appeared with delicious Egyptian bread stuffed with fried beans and salad. Amy almost felt like one of the team as she sat on the rocky ground to talk about the work so far . . . and what they hoped to discover that afternoon, when the X-ray visions would begin.

Although high metal fences had been set up around the entrance to the Cat Tomb, she still hoped to catch a glimpse of what was happening on this site. Not a hope. There was a gate in the fence but no one went in, no one came out.

She fingered the little limestone cat picture that she still carried with her . . . and found herself talking to it. 'Not yet,' she said. 'I can't go in there yet. You'll have to wait.'

# 15 Sentry Duty

*For I am Seth who can raise a tumult of storm in the horizon of the sky . . . one whose will is destruction . . .*
*(Book of the Dead)*

The day would end in blood, but it began simply enough. Yet another tour of sentry duty. Walk the bank. Spy on Deshret. Report anything unusual.

Each day Shabti kicked dust as he marched from the compound and through the fields to the river. Here the cooling breeze blew some of his resentment away. The soil became lovely and mushy underfoot. No whips, no dogs, no arrogant aristocrats here. Frogs gossiped from the reed beds and when he stooped to wash his face he saw countless tadpoles wiggling. Sparrows chattered, lapwings peeped and ducks quacked comfortably. Flies buzzed, giant jewel-coloured dragonflies hovered nearby and the annoying wasp at his ear still droned on. No. Wait. He held his breath and listened. He no longer heard the wasp. Small mercies!

Occasionally he passed other servants of Kemet. None of them spoke to him or bothered to watch him pass. Some worked the wooden *shaduf* – the clever wooden beam designed to help draw water from the river. Others balanced on reed boats, hauling nets of shimmering fish.

He smirked. He had his own fish – a full pouch of food and a leather bottle of tangy barley beer. Hob had agreed to that much. No more thieving! Better still, he could now start planning how to get supplies together for his escape through the invisible hole.

'I'll soon be free!' he called to the blue sky and the green reeds. His words sounded thin. Only the crocodile opened one round eye at the sound of them.

Even after three days on patrol he still couldn't puzzle out the pattern of the land. He understood the river, that was simple – it flowed. He understood the fields – they were ploughed, sown and reaped. What he couldn't possibly see was how he could slog along with the river on his right, the fields on his left, and yet the sun would always be straight ahead. The white house was always dead centre of the fields. Surely this ought to mean he was travelling in a circle? But the river didn't curve round, save for the occasional gentle meander. He couldn't explain how else it should have been, he just knew it was all *wrong*. Everything was wrong! He knew he was out of place, that he wasn't used to the work or solitude. Could he remember having servants of his own once? Being part of a crowd of laughing, bragging boys?

No sign of them now.

He knew no songs to sing, had no one to tell stories to. He amused himself instead scratching lines in the dirt with a stick. This soon palled, but he had an idea for something better. One evening he gathered a few pieces of stone from a pile of rubble that had been swept up after the earthquake in the compound. He picked out a couple of flakes of limestone that were smooth enough and flat enough for what he wanted. When he saw workers touching up the paintwork on a newly plastered hut he snaffled a cake of brown pigment. It was easy to find a quiet spot on the riverbank where he could grind the paint to powder, using the hollow of a freshwater clam shell. He mixed in some drops of water, watched it coalesce, then stirred.

He'd seen scribes working for Hob, making an inventory of each day's harvest. For pens they used reeds, which grew in abundance along the full stretch of the river, so, like them, he chewed the stalk of a reed and twisted the fibres to create a brush. Making lines was strangely exhilarating. Perhaps he'd once learned how to paint, in the time before Kemet? He quickly covered one flake of stone with dabs of paint and there was King the cat, standing on his hind paws, ordering little mice to nibble the invisible hole. Somehow he dredged deep memories to draw a column of writing at the side of his cartoon, saying 'I am the Great Tom Cat!' He didn't sign his work. That never occurred to him. Besides, he didn't have any idea what name to put.

As the paint dried he grazed his fingertips over the picture of the cat.

*What are you always trying to tell me? What is it you're trying to get me to do?*

Reaching for the second fragment of limestone he paused for a moment, wondering what to draw next. Hob's grotesque twists of hair? Lines of geese waddling across the compound? Or the grey heron, taking in twilight from the roof of the white house?

His thoughts turned to Lady Anhai. He didn't think any brush stroke could be fine enough to give a true impression of her ethereal presence, or any paint so faint. As he pictured her in his mind, a shape leaped out. It was the dull eye jewel she wore from a golden loop around her neck. Only, he couldn't help imagining it brighter, glittering with turquoise, emerald and lapis lazuli . . . Disgusted that he only had the colour brown, he threw the stones and paints away. Time to get walking again, get kicking at pebbles and picking at patchy memories.

One thing remained constant through all his hours of sentry duty – he never escaped the nasty prickle of awareness that Deshret's barren expanse was close. The heat from the desert began to stoke the flame of rebelliousness he felt burning inside him. He decided he wanted a clear view over the haze of desert and the misshapen mountains in the distance. He wanted to know what it was about Deshret that made Hob so nervous.

Coming to a low rise, he stood up tall and shaded his eyes against the sun's glare, staring directly across the river.

*Show me what you've got!* was his challenge.

He gazed for a long while. It was almost familiar, this poise, this concentration.

*Have I scouted before?* he wondered. Had there been a time when he was on patrol, perhaps even on the edge of desert lands? His hand made a fist voluntarily, not to punch, but as if he wanted to hold something. A hoe?

No, not a common digging tool! At that moment he sensed the ghost of a weapon in his hand. A spear, perhaps? Long and straight, with a sharp bright point on the end for driving *hard* into a target. If not a spear, he wanted a bow.

*What's a bow?*

He couldn't have explained it in words, but his hand and arm remembered the feel of a lightweight wooden bow, strung taut, ready to be fired.

*What at?*

Was there a flicker of movement in Deshret's red desert? Did something skitter across the gritty dunes? He was too far away to see. On the far bank of the river was a mound of rocks. They'd make a perfect promontory for spying out the land, if he could just swim across and climb up there . . .

Movement again. It was too frustrating to get these hints and flickers of life beyond the river! If he was going to be a proper sentry he had to know what was out there. More to the point, he had to know if it was still going to be possible to escape Kemet, whether through the invisible hole, or across the wastes of Deshret.

*I* will *cross the river*, he told himself.

At first he was fine. The water was as cool as he remembered it. Tiny insects clouded the air and there were shimmering ripples as water rats dived into the water alongside him. A pair of plump ducks swam part of the way with him. One dragonfly even landed on his head for a moment, before its wings whirred again and carried it off to a clump of papyrus plants.

About halfway across the river something changed. It was as if the water had become a current of sludge, as if his legs were made of mud, as if his arms were weak hanks of wool.

*I will make it across!*

A tremendous burst of anger kept him moving. How dare anyone forbid him anything? How dare Lady Anhai treat him as if he were a brainless peasant! He was *strong*, he was *proud*, he could do anything he liked! Once he'd held a bow! Once he'd fired arrows at coppery targets and cowering prey!

This pride and self-glory kept his head above water and his limbs struggling against the spell of Hob's command not to leave Kemet. He seemed to draw strength from the sun's long rays. Stroke by stroke he conquered the river, step by stumbling step he crawled up on to the far bank, only to collapse from the effort. He'd made it. Now anything was possible.

There were no ducks in Deshret. No friendly sparrows gossiped here. No fluffy seed heads tickled him as they floated by. Nothing grew in Deshret. Nothing could. Even after a few moments he felt the intense heat dragging away all his energy.

He pulled himself up the nearby crag, one boulder at a time. The red granite rock sparkled beautifully but tore at his bare skin. Corners of his mind showed him images of tall towers made of the same red stone – *obelisks*, they were called. He remembered impassive statues and painted columns, a whole town, in fact. Had that been *home*?

Having pushed Hob's spell off his shoulders, now it seemed as if his mind were becoming clearer, as if there were more room for memories.

First he had to get a proper view of the world. He peered across the desert. The haze was even stronger on this side of the river. It was impossible to focus on anything. From time to time he'd be startled by the sight of sudden dust devils whipped up in the sand. Abruptly the shapes would collapse, only to spout up again in a completely different direction.

*Stop trying so hard*, a voice said in his mind. *Let your instinct take over. You've done this hundreds of times before. Stand still in the centre of the world and let all your senses suck details in . . .*

He all but closed his eyes and dragged in breath after

breath of rough air. Then he emptied his lungs and let his body go calm. There was nothing but sun, rock and sand. He was part of it all.

*What can I see?*

Although the desert of Deshret seemed to be a wide open space, his senses now crawled with the certainty that it was not empty. It was crowded with an aggression so dense and dangerous it nearly pushed him backwards off the boulder. Where before there had been nothing but dust eddies and heat haze, now he saw scaled skin writhing, teeth bared in wide jaws and eyes flashing malevolence. Even as he watched, two terrifying shapes reared up mountain-high. One was lithe and green, snake-like; the other wild and deformed, with crocodile teeth and lion's hair. Both hideous creatures were bloated with power, ready to strike and devour him . . .

With a cry he jumped down from the rock. Streaks of shadow passed over him. He crouched low with his arms wrapped round his head, not ashamed to tremble. Then another sound made him lift his pale face. It was a deep bellow of pain and outrage. Where was it coming from? Somewhere further ahead in the river . . .

He waded into the shallows and began to move cautiously towards the noise. Hob said to report anything unusual. Was it unusual to see the normally placid water churning up like a bubbling pot? Was it normal to see the great white hippopotamus writhing in a storm of pain? What had happened?

That question was quickly answered. He saw great black spear ends sticking out from the animal's massive sides. Even as he watched, another spear came cutting through the air to pierce the hippo's shoulder. Dark red blood welled out. Shabti was mesmerized.

It was as if he'd seen this all before – the hippo thrashing in the river, the line of a spear thrown true to target, the gobbets of blood. He'd heard the anguished bellows and seen the waves of reddened water as prey roiled and recoiled. Yes, he'd hunted before. He'd been on another river, slinking through the reeds on a papyrus boat, with heavy spears trailing fat ropes. The ropes were for hauling exhausted hippos to the shore once they were bled of energy and aggression. Had he really once enjoyed such sport? Had he never heard the bellows of pain from the wounded animals – all the antelopes, hares, lions and foxes skewered for fun by his mirror-bright spearheads?

No. He'd heard only the baying of his hunting hounds, the hooves of his horses and the song of the wind rushing by. There'd been a chariot, he knew that now. There was something bad about the chariot. Something too appalling to remember. Pain, pain and more pain. Agony like the final moments of the wounded hippopotamus.

More spears came hurtling out of Deshret. He was ashamed he could do nothing to stop them. Stupidly he splashed through the water, waving his arms, shouting until his voice was hoarse, 'Leave her alone! Leave her alone!'

The hippopotamus slumped.

Shabti waded as close as he dared.

He counted at least twenty spears and wondered if he should pull them out. He was afraid this would make the blood run more freely. Already the wonderful white hue of the hippo's hide was fading. Fine black lines were spreading across it, like the fronds of a fanning marsh plant. The creature made a tremendous effort to drag her wounded body up on to the muddy bank. She succeeded in getting her head out of the water then collapsed for a final time. There was nothing Shabti could do but squat down nearby and watch the mighty ribs push out and in as she drew her last few breaths.

'You can't die,' he whispered. 'You're the first thing I ever saw when I woke up in Kemet. You're strong. Keep fighting!'

Slowly the hippo opened her jaws and showed her

fearsome array of teeth. For a moment he thought she would lunge forward and bite. She didn't. She gave a sad groan and reluctantly lay low. Her eyes stayed open. He was forced to watch as the light in their depths dwindled . . . flickered . . . and went out all together. Then she was gone. Only the carcase remained, nothing but a weighty lump with blood drying in dark rivulets.

He felt like tearing out a spear and flinging it into the desert. He even thought he'd like to hurl *himself* at Deshret in defiance. But he didn't move. He was lost in another memory, seeing a different river scene . . .

Himself in fine clothes with dogs and servants, a spear in hand. A hippo, smaller than this one and brown, not white. A common fisherman daring to wave his hands in protest: *No, no, there's a young one*. The warning merited only a cruel smile.

In his mind Shabti relived the moment when he tested the weight of his spear and set himself to defy one of the most dangerous beasts in the country. So it was defending a baby? That would make the fight more exciting! Ordering his servants to follow his lead, he baited and bullied the brown hippo until it was pure fury. Then he struck it between the eyes, piercing the brain with one brilliant throw.

He remembered the feeling of excitement and

jubilation – how his servants had clapped when he'd turned his face to the sun as if to say, *Look at me! See what I've done!* He'd only laughed when men chased the fat baby hippo out of its hiding place. It had waddled over to its mother's still body, nudging and nuzzling it long after the sun went down and shadows turned everything cold.

Remembering this, Shabti went as grey as twilight.

*Was that me? Was that the sort of boy I was?*

Another black spear came whizzing over his head, piercing the river.

He came to his senses. Bundling all of his fear and shame into a hard lump deep inside, he began to swim again, this time away from Deshret to Kemet's green shore. He dived for the spear on the way and rose out of the water with it gripped in his fist. Reaching land he ran until his lungs were on fire.

'Deshret comes! They attack! Where are you?' he called, pushing his way through fields of flax and barley.

This time it was Master Hob who answered, 'Here I am!'

# 16 The Mystery Boy

*A heart has throbbed beneath that leathern breast*
*And tears down that dusty cheek have roll'd.*

(Horace Smith)

'Who are you?'

Amy mouthed the words from behind her cotton face mask.

She was staring down at the white-sheeted body, lifted free from the stone sarcophagus and resting now on a fabric stretcher, like a car crash victim waiting too long for an ambulance. She found herself horribly drawn to the mummy, with its bright ceramic eyes and white teeth glowing next to old brown skin. What would it say if it could speak to her now? Why did she have the feeling that there was something to communicate? Something waiting to be done?

All the while she looked at it, she was fingering the warm limestone in her pocket.

It was strange to think that with X-rays and CAT scans they could see through the scraps of mottled linen to the body inside. Stranger still to know it had once been a living, moving human, before death stole the warmth and breath away. All that time spent growing as a person, learning things, experiencing life, storing up memories, then, *bam!* in a few seconds death stole it all away and only the husk remained.

Not something you wanted to see first-hand. Not something you could ever forget if you had. Not something she ought to brood over now.

Time itself was strange, she thought. Wide enough to separate centuries and yet somehow able to be folded so that ancient and modern could touch.

'Don't touch! Not without gloves.'

She jumped at the sound of Ellie's warning and pulled her hand back. 'I didn't realize I was . . . Sorry.'

'Not a pretty sight, eh?'

It was horrible, but sad, too – that people would spend all that time and effort trying to live for ever when death was so unavoidable. She asked Ellie, 'Don't you get, you know, depressed, doing archaeology? I mean, everything you find is dead – dead people's houses or pots or stuff or bodies.'

Ellie shook her head. 'I see it more as bringing things to life, imagining people in the houses, making the pots, wandering around in their bodies.'

'Except you can't bring people back to life. When they're dead they're gone. For good. It's stupid trying to pretend they're not!'

She hadn't meant to speak so loudly. Even Dan heard her through the din of the music in his earphones.

Ellie gave her a curious look. 'That's why we try to make so much of being alive while we can,' she said. 'Live while you're alive and all that.'

Amy turned away.

'Very philosophical,' Rosa interrupted, dismissing the emotions thickening the hot air of the tiny chamber. 'All we need to remember now is that the ancient Egyptians loved life so much they wanted to live for ever, and this mummy here is proof of that. Now, if you're staying close to the X-ray machine you'll need one of these blue lead aprons on.'

Dan and Ellie arranged the digital detector and the portable X-ray tubes, which were held up by a sturdy aluminium frame. A beam of red light traced the mummy's contours. One press of a button captured a static image that was relayed to the computer screen. A series of images were taken to build up a complete picture of the remains.

'In the nineteenth century they would have had a grand public unwrapping of mummies,' Ellie murmured to Amy. 'Quite a big spectacle, selling tickets and all that.'

'Right. And now we do it for TV and *Action Archaeology!* makes a fortune.'

'We'll begin at the head,' said Rosa. 'X-ray images won't show soft tissue, we have the CAT scan for that, later, but we can clearly see evidence of how the brain was removed by inserting a tool into the nose, breaking the ethmoid bone, at this point here. This dense object here, in the nose, is most probably a piece of wood, placed in the nose to keep the shape.'

Amy's eyes widened. She'd read about it, fascinated by grisly descriptions of how the brain was whisked up, then how it poured from the nose like lumpy grey snot.

'. . . The brain matter itself would be discarded as irrelevant. We know that the *heart* was considered the home of intelligence, and generally left in the body ready for when the *ba* of the mummy had to face judgement in the underworld.'

Amy felt her own heart beat uncomfortably as X-ray images showed even more breakages to the skull.

Once more Rosa spoke the language of science. 'Maxilla and mandible whole, fractures to the left occipital and parietal bones . . .'

It didn't take an expert to see that the bones of the skull were badly damaged. Rosa explained that the damage could be pre- or post-mortem. Before or after death. It was possibly from careless handling by embalmers, or caused when tomb robbers searched the corpse for valuables.

A new image appeared on the computer screen. A skeleton's grin.

'The teeth are in excellent condition,' said Rosa. 'Very little attrition, meaning they're hardly worn at all. That suggests a diet of good quality food, not bread made from gritty flour contaminated with sand. These dental caries may have been painful, though. These teeth here needed fillings. Probably too much honey in the food.'

There was more specialist vocabulary about tooth eruption rates, canines, incisors and molars. Amy only really understood what was going on when she heard Rosa finish with very chilling words. 'All of the dental evidence suggests someone aged between ten-and-a-half and twelve years old. A child.'

A child!

That was a very unwelcome and unsettling discovery. Suddenly the body looked more vulnerable, less like an anonymous grotesquery. Amy thought of kids at school, a few years below her, slouching along the corridors with overstuffed bags banging against their legs and school uniforms all awry.

Only Kev looked pleased. He said finding a mummified child made great TV.

Dan moved the detector plates and the examination continued with the chest. Amy didn't like looking at pictures of broken ribs. She knew from experience how painful they felt. Then the X-ray moved down to the abdomen.

Rosa pointed to a thin slit in the mummy's belly. 'This is where the intestines and other internal organs are usually drawn out and placed in their canopic jars.'

Filming stopped as Ellie said, 'There weren't any jars found on site. In fact, there wasn't much of anything found on site, thanks to thieves, the flood damage and subsidence. We've no way of knowing if the squidgy bits were embalmed separately.'

Rosa was confused. 'Squidgy bits? Is that a Yorkshire expression?'

'No, sorry! Just a short way of saying, liver, lungs, stomach and guts.'

'Not a technical term, then? But descriptive! The CAT scans will confirm if any major organs were left in the body. Could you pass me the tweezers again Amy? I'll take samples to be analyzed later. We'll be able to tell if alcohol or date palm oil was used to sterilize the body cavity, as well as testing for the presence of natron salts.'

For drying out the body, Amy thought. Books about Egyptian mummification were being brought to life with a vengeance now.

Rosa continued. 'This X-ray image clearly shows a dense mass of packing in the abdominal area. I would say bundles of linen soaked in natron, though mud is sometimes used. The endoscopy will give us a clearer view.'

Amy's expression said, *Endo what?*

Ellie obliged. 'Fibre optic tube for looking inside things.'

'Now,' said Rosa, 'as we examine the pelvic girdle, we can perhaps decide if the child is female or male. The sciatic notch, *here* on the image, this is quite shallow, not flared out for future childbirth, which tells us it is probably a boy. We can also look further at the ends of the arm and leg bones, where bone growth called *epiphyses* takes place. This growth gradually hardens with age, so we can confirm that . . . Oh!'

The scientist was, for the first time that day, a little flustered.

Kev asked them all to wait up while he changed the camera batteries.

Amy looked at the image relayed from the X-ray. What had made Rosa stop like that? 'Is there something wrong?'

Ellie moved in closer to Rosa. She whistled. 'Now I see why the left leg is slightly shorter than the right. Blimey, that's a *massive* injury on the left hip. Look, Amy, the thigh's been severely dislocated – actually wrenched out of the socket joint and jammed back against the pelvic bone.'

'Oh dear.' Rosa murmured something in Arabic.

'Oh dear *what*?' Amy didn't like the sound of anything so ominous. It reminded her of her own still-aching injuries.

'This dense mass shows where the damage began to heal.'

'That's good, isn't it?'

Rosa shook her head. 'The child lived for a short while after the breakage but he would have been in terrible pain. Agony. The compound fracture here in the left femur – the thigh bone – suggests some kind of accident.'

'Compound fracture?'

'When the bone breaks the skin,' Ellie explained. 'It's the most dangerous sort because the wound can suppurate. Think, blood poisoning and stinky pus. Eventually gangrene would get so bad the leg could need amputating – we know the Egyptians had the knowledge of how to do that.'

'Well, his leg obviously wasn't cut off,' Amy said, 'so maybe he didn't get gangrene after all.'

'No,' said Rosa grimly, 'The boy didn't live long enough for that to happen. We can only hope he was heavily drugged – with opium probably – to dull the pain. It must have been a very bad accident, to cause so much trauma.'

Oh. Lovely. 'You know what? I'm gonna get some air . . .'

Amy scrambled up the tunnel towards the light. She wished the hot sun could scour her clean inside and out, scrub away all memories of the boy in the tomb, of his accident, of all accidents . . .

She came face to face with the bare metal fence round the Cat Tomb. The entrance gate was ajar, wide enough for Farouk's men to drag away old car tyres filled with rubble. Wide enough to see through. See what? A white shirt and blue jeans. Jason Henderson. He stood in her way, blocking her view inside the enclosure.

'Amy! Are you all done in the Chariot Tomb? Find anything good? Hey, are you OK? D'you want to sit down? Have a drink? Shall I fetch your dad?'

'Dad?'

There he was in front of her, and she was hiding in his big shadow. A wind was blowing in her ear and her lips were wet with warm water. When her head stopped spinning she realized Jason was squatting at her side, wafting her with a wadge of paper. Spots of water glistened on the wool of her jumper.

Her dad was waving a half-empty bottle at her. 'Can't you take that wool thing off, Munchkin? You must be baking. No wonder you fainted!'

Fainted? Had she really done that? Ugh, did that mean Jason had caught her?

'I'm fine,' she said, but her voice was croaky.

'Got a bit stuffy down there, did it? Here, grab Jason's arm, he'll take you down to the shelter.' Dad patted her cheek, gave her an encouraging grin, and flapped his hands. 'Shoo, shoo – go cool down.'

Amy shrugged Jason away. 'I really am fine.'

'It's too hot for you.'

'I *know* it's hot! I'll go sit in the shelter and drink a million gallons of water, only would you all just leave me alone?'

'Consider yourself left.'

She knew they were watching her go. She could hear broken sentences following her down the slope.

'Poor girl,' said Dad. 'All a bit much for her, after the accident, you know . . .'

'. . . accident?'

'Mm. Best we don't . . .'

'. . . didn't know . . .'

'. . . terrible tragedy . . . no miscarriage from the shock news, thank God . . . due after Christmas . . .'

'Claire's boyfriend . . . ?'

'. . . nothing they could do. Dead at the scene. Heigh ho . . . Back to work.'

*Accident.*

Amy's brain sloshed with thoughts, as if someone was stirring it up with an invisible whisk. She half expected it to come pouring out somewhere.

What if the boy in the tomb had been in a traffic accident too? Not a car crash, of course. Not the swerve, screech, smash, crash, silence of cars crumpling. No mobile phones ringing uselessly or rain falling across slanted headlights. No, forget that. Think of the Egyptian equivalent.

An after-image of a faded painting sped before her eyes.

Had the boy been mangled in a chariot crash?


When the sun sank low and the cliffs were blushed with pink and orange, the two archaeological teams were ready to leave. Farouk left men on guard, with the dog Anubis for company – and protection.

Amy wanted to ask Ellie something, but she was chatting with Rosa Hassan, so she had to sit next to Jason instead.

'Are you feeling better now?'

She ignored his concern. She'd had enough sickly compassion the last couple of months. Enough of girls like Charlotte Pratt gushing, *But are you really all right, Amy, you don't look it?* Instead she asked, 'Do you know anything about chariots?'

'What about them?'

'Not the chariots exactly. I mean, who used them?'

He thought about it for a moment. 'Tony said the Egyptians nicked the idea for chariots off these guys called the Hykssos, who'd invaded Egypt. By the nineteenth dynasty – when our two tombs were probably built – the Hykssos had been kicked out of the country but the pharaohs thought they ought to use chariots in battle, to give superiority.'

'OK, but did boys ride them?'

'There were these guys, young lads, called the *Maryannu*. The Young Heroes. They were a sort of elite fighting squad.'

'And they'd have to be rich to afford chariots? The sort of rich where you'd get a rocky tomb like the one we found?'

'Oh yes. Spoilt rich kids, probably. One ancient scribe wrote that the Young Heroes used to go hurtling around showing off their expensive kit. *Youth of today, grow their hair too long and drive their chariots too fast*, that sort of thing. Why'd you ask?'

'Dunno.'

She shrugged. Why would she care what happened to a shrivelled-up mummy from thousands of years before? Why was Egypt making her feel so wrenched away from her own life . . . so drawn to the ground underneath the paw of the limestone cat?

'Too bad we don't know the kid's name,' she said suddenly, but Jason had turned away.

# 17 Attack from the Red Land

*Lift up your faces, you soldiers of Ra!*

*(Book of the Dead)*

Shabti gripped his new spear. His eyes were fierce and he was ready to fight. One false move, one flicker of distraction, and the dogs would spring. Rip lunged and snapped just out of reach of the spear tip, which was purpled with some kind of poison. Bite was more cunning. He kept his belly low and his yellow eyes fixed on the boy's bare legs.

Shabti squared his shoulders and measured the distance to the target he'd chosen – the unfolding lotus flower carved on to Lady Anhai's garden gate. This, *this* was what he was meant to do. This was what he had known before the gruelling slavery of Kemet.

Memories were very close.

Day after day of rigorous training, running, wrestling, boxing, hurling spears, firing deadly arrows. And the horses! He smiled to remember the exhilarating speed of his two war steeds, shining with sweat and gleaming metal tack. On and on his chariot had raced, scorning rocks and ruts, matching every gust of wind. His head recalled the pressure of his leather helmet; he knew the familiarity of the spear's weight in his hand. He'd see a target, gauge the throw, arm back, aim true, then . . . hurl! The long javelin would speed home – *thud*.

He took in a big gulp of air and realized he wasn't in a chariot, racing his rivals. He was barefoot and ragged in a dusty compound. He threw the spear anyway, sending it with such force and resentment that the wooden lotus was split right across the centre and the spear cracked too. The impact of his throw made the gate swing open. Garden perfumes drifted out. He wished Lady Anhai could have been there to see his skill. To admire him for it. More intensely than ever he thought of the invisible hole in the garden – his secret way of escape back to proper pride and glory.

'Show me!' Hob's voice rasped across the boy's daydreams. 'Show me where you found that spear.'

*

The white hippopotamus lay exactly where she'd fallen.

Hob stared at the carcass. Barbs jutted obscenely from her hide. Her eyes were still glassy and open. A flock of coarse black birds with stabbing beaks had settled on her flesh. Little sparrows whirled through the air, all out of harmony.

Rip and Bite hurtled into the brown water of the river, choking as they tried to bark and swim at the same time. The birds flew off, every last feather, though the carrion-eaters landed again in Deshret, not so far away. Shabti sensed they weren't the only things that watched from the red wasteland.

Turning to give Hob a smug *told you so*, he was amazed to see raw grief on that harsh face. Hob's sadness soon solidified to anger.

'The abominations dare too much!' he shouted. 'Always I've kept my eye on them – two eyes recently. Now they dare do this! They'll not cross the river though. That's not how things are. Demons dwell in Deshret and Kemet is the land of Lady Anhai. We keep the balance. This is a land of abundance and they are creatures of sand and rock. They'll taunt us, murder whatever they can with their foul weapons, but they'll never cross the river. Never.'

Wordlessly Shabti pointed some way downstream of the dead hippo. Instead of flowing smoothly, the water and blood slowed to frothy pools that slowly spilled over a new-formed dam.

Rocks in the river? There were no rocks in the river!

Hob marched over. 'Did you put those there, boy? Thinking of escaping across to the red land, eh?'

'Do you think I could lift anything so heavy with these starved arms? Look there, where the sunlight reflects on the far bank. That's where the rocks have fallen from. There's another one ready to tumble now.'

'The earthquake must have shaken them loose.'

'The earth isn't quaking now and the rock's still rolling towards the river.'

Hob actually whipped round and whacked Shabti across the face. 'Be quiet! You don't know what you're talking about.'

'It's falling now!'

Shabti could barely focus, his head reeled so soundly from Hob's blow. He saw, or thought he saw, a cluster of jerky figures on the shore of Deshret. They were pressing hands, legs, shoulders and claws up against the boulder. When he blinked sweat and blood from his eyes the vision vanished. The rock remained teetering . . . teetering . . . rolling down, *splash* into the water.

One more stepping stone across the river.

That wasn't the worst of it.

A worker came trotting through the flax fields. Her face was crumpled with anxiety.

'Reniseb sent me, Master Hob. She says to tell you the water's failing. Our channels won't fill. The salad plants are dying and we've nothing to give them.'

Hob said, 'There must be a minor earth fall in one of the dykes. You know how to clear those.'

'No, Master Hob, there's no blockage . . . and no water!'

Shabti looked from the worker to the river full of rocks. The monsters must be clever – to dam water meant for the food!

Hob guessed what the boy was thinking. He swore so violently it even made the dogs whimper.

'Come. We'll see for ourselves.'

Perhaps there once had been balance in Kemet but now it was definitely teetering. Once again Shabti wondered why he felt as if he had some part to play in righting things, when surely he had nothing to do with upsetting them. He couldn't – or wouldn't – remember any crime so bad it would upset Anhai's world in this way.

The overseer Reniseb cringed to see Hob approach. 'It's as I told you, I've had them out here tilling the square salad patches, the same as every day, only now the lettuces . . . look at them . . .'

Once lush plants were now nothing but flat green streaks on hot earth. Any radish tops showing above the soil had dried and split. The leeks were wilting and the onions were shrivelled to papery layers.

'If the water channels are blocked, what about the *shaduf*?' Hob growled. 'Get the men dipping that in the river – that's what it's for.'

'It wouldn't raise more than a few buckets, the river's so low. Nowhere near enough to keep the dykes full and the fields green.'

Shabti looked into the nearest irrigation channel, then out over the whole network. It was dry – they were all dry, or showing only meagre streaks of damp at the bottom, speckled with the flapping bodies of small fish.

*Can't we save the fish?* he thought, and that surprised him.

Time was he'd never even have noticed such small life forms, let alone wished them well. Once, he remembered, he'd leaped down from his chariot and crushed a scarab beetle under one sandal. It had been busy rolling a ball of eggs in dried earth and dung. He'd kicked the dung away contemptuously, not caring if the eggs hatched or died.

Now here he was, heavy-hearted at the slaughter of a mere hippo, at the last contortions of dying fish, at the wilting stalks of overripe wheat. What was happening to him? This was no way for a young hero to be! Would it help him ride faster, throw further or fight more fiercely? No! He was, or had been, above such soft feelings. One of the Young Heroes, yes, that's what they'd been called. Boys in a blaze of glory.

On and on the chariot in his memory raced. Dust clouds clung to his skin. Was that something on the road ahead? A procession? Let it shift, and shift quickly, he wasn't going to stop! Was that something following behind? Now his skin prickled and he whipped round, feeling as if all the malice of Deshret was burning into him and him alone.

'Boy! D'you want me to knock the fluff out of your head again?' Hob gave him an ungentle shake and made him snap back to present time.

'Get the workers back to the compound,' Hob yelled at Reniseb. 'It's not safe here.'

'It won't be safe there,' Shabti blurted out.

'What did you say?'

'I mean, it won't be safe there, *Master Hob*.'

'No, what did you *mean*? Do you know something you're not telling me, dung bag?'

'I don't *know* anything, except they've dammed the river and made a bridge. They must mean to cross over it.'

'All the more reason to get back to safety.'

Hob spoke with his usual gruffness but his voice betrayed hesitancy. Fear, even.

Shabti turned his back on Deshret and looked out over the crops to where the grey heron preened on the white house roof. Did Lady Anhai have any idea of the danger she was in? Would she even care if she knew? Not that it mattered. Let her keep her head in the sand . . . the clouds . . . wherever she went to hide from realities.

'Call all the overseers together,' he said firmly. 'I don't see why we have to sit and wait to be skewered. There are plans we can make, things we can do . . .'

Yes, and while other people were busy doing them, there would be plenty of time to slip away in search of his own safety. He'd be through that hidden hole and free!

They began massing at sunset, the unseen monsters. Work stopped in Kemet. Where there had been frantic labours and fast whips cracking, now there was only an uncomfortable silence. The cows did not low and the dogs did not bark.

'Why can't we see the damn things?' Hob whispered.

'It's like they're made of dust and dry heat!'

*Maybe they are*, Shabti thought. Maybe they were the other side of the balance. Kemet was a land of life and abundance, Deshret meant death and desolation. Now the balance was shifting, what sort of catastrophe could occur?

Only as the sun's glad light faded did they catch sight of red-stained shapes on the ridge of the riverbank.

Hob and Shabti – impromptu generals – were crouching behind the low wall of a roof-top drying space. Behind them rows of sheets hung forlorn.

'Leave them!' Shabti ordered.

The laundry overseer was a thin man called Keben. He had a face like a long fish, and he went into a flap at the mere suggestion.

'But everything should be folded and stored!'

'If there's a breeze they'll move and distract enemy aim from us, which is good.'

'But my lady needs her linens!'

'Your lady has chests full of clothes she can't possibly wear all at once.'

'But we always take the washing down at sunset, then we fold it and we lay it in baskets and . . .'

'Not any more!' said Shabti. 'Don't you people understand? None of that matters. Honestly, you act as if serving Lady Anhai was the only thing you were ever made for. Do you think those Deshret monsters care about your stupid routines and safe little slave ways? I'm amazed you've even done what I've told you to defend this place. If I hadn't made any plans you'd all be sitting snug in the Night House while your world was torn apart! If you want to do anything with those sheets, rip them into bandages.'

'What for?'

'What for?! Do I have to explain everything? For when you *bleed*!'

Keben gaped. 'Bleed? We don't bleed.'

'Of course you do, when you cut yourself working, or fall and graze yourself, when Hob goes after you with that whip!' Shabti pointed to his gallery of wounds, all in different stages of healing or bruising.

Hob muscled in. He took a wicked sharp knife from his kilt top and drew a line on his arm. The skin parted. No blood welled out.

'What about them?' Shabti asked, looking to where shadows gathered. 'Can *they* be made to bleed?'

As if on cue a dreadful noise rose up from the river edge. A festering moan at first, rupturing to a growl then gritting the air with a howl as dry as grated rock.

Keben fled.

After that things happened so quickly the very sky

seemed to boil with action. Nets caught the first wave of invaders. They'd crossed the dwindling river on boulder bridges, whooping and shrieking with dismay to be so near water. Fighting complaints of *It's not what we usually do*, Shabti had persuaded Lady Anhai's fishermen to hide their nets in the river reeds. No birds or fish were snared, only invisible creatures that made the coarse nets writhe as if with life of their own. *Gnash*, *gnash* – teeth gnawed. The nets split and the reeds were trampled under gnarly feet.

Shabti had hoped to slow them down for longer, but at least it gave the enemy something to think about.

By then the sun was well and truly gone. Everything beyond the compound was in darkness. He found it agony to crouch low, keening the air for sounds of attack. He was waiting for the perfect moment to slip away to his secret hole, where no monsters would follow. So why didn't he get up and go right away? Why didn't he act on the fear growing deep inside? Why should he worry about what the monsters wanted, or who they hunted?

Because he had something to do. Someone to save . . . Someone who scorned the very sight of him and kept aloof in her house.

\* \* \*

The enemy advanced in leaps and lurches. In darkness they came, crashing through the fields. Everywhere they walked or crawled, the crops crumbled to grey ash. The very ground groaned and split, drying out to crusts and scabs. Crickets, beetles, birds in their eggs, everything died that couldn't escape.

Hob was impatient. 'I'll send the signal now.'

'No, wait.'

'I said, I'll send it *now*.'

'And I said, *wait*. They aren't close enough yet.'

'They're close.'

'Not close enough,' Shabti replied through gritted teeth. 'Listen.'

'Listen? One more word of insolence from you, runt, and I'll have the dogs rip your tongue out'

Soon, sooner than he'd hoped, Shabti heard the sign he'd been waiting for. Live geese had been collared and staked in the fields. They'd been happy enough at first, pecking the ground and preening feathers. When the sun set they must have sensed that something sinister was about to happen, and when danger was actually upon them they hissed and honked with amazing energy. The sound of their warning carried to the compound. Then necks were snapped and warm bodies trampled.

'*Now* they're close enough. Send the signal now.'

Hob whistled once. He was answered by Keben in the yard below. The message spread from one worker to another until orange light split the air. Reniseb was out in the fields, holding a flaming torch aloft. Her hair had come loose from its plaits. The ends frizzled and burned as they wafted too close to the fire.

Fire was Shabti's idea. He'd remembered how his lamp of kikki oil had illuminated the secret chamber.

As soon as the torch dipped low, new fire raced out along shallow channels filled with oil. Flames stretched up as if trying to seize its own black, stinking smoke. Hob was mesmerized. He couldn't believe the runt-boy's plan was actually working! He leaned forward, eyes shining as much as the new light. Was he seeing straight? Was it his imagination? Were the flames somehow distorting? They certainly didn't burn true. The orange and red tongues began to lick new spikes and bulges. The heat hardened into arms, legs, tails and teeth.

'Sun save us,' Hob murmured. 'I can actually see them in the fire.'

First one then seemingly thousands of creatures stepped across the firewall. At the moment of crossing their bodies showed up clearly, flame-coloured and fearsome. Shabti couldn't drag his gaze away. Such horrors! Goblins, demons, dark spirits – he didn't know what they were, nor could he count the weapons each grotesquery brandished. Their eyes seered white like the heart of the fire, then dimmed to charcoal black. On and on the creatures came, rank after rank, crossing the fire though it charred and burned, releasing a holocaust of howls.

It wasn't the general deformity that made Shabti shake with fear. It wasn't even the fiery glint of the clashing blades. Something far worse rose from the smoke of the firewall, something with scales that shone like blood-red rubies. Something with a mouthful of teeth and a mane of fire. A monster lurching straight out of a nightmare.

'What is that thing?' Shabti whispered to Hob, who shook his head slowly.

'Nothing Deshret has spawned before. It looks as if it would devour the sky with one mouthful.'

At the nightmare's side was a hideous coiling snake.

'Apophis,' Hob gagged. 'That I *have* heard of. The Serpent of Chaos. No man can fight that!'

Shabti could only stand and watch as both monsters lurched through the fire. A web of fear strangled his heart. *Run now!* The fear screamed. *Run while there's still time, while you've still breath in your lungs and blood in your body. This fight's not yours, this war's not of your making. Run, just run!*

# 18 Midnight under the Stars

*Be merry all your life;*
*Toil no more than is required,*
*Nor cut short the time allotted for pleasure . . .*
(Instructions to Ptahhotep, *c.* 2350 BC)

Christmas Eve on the edge of the desert.

Instead of waddling down a rain-slick high street in England with Claire, loaded with last-minute presents, thick coats and woollies, Amy spent the day at the *souk* in Luxor. She sniffed at bowls of spices, drank the scent of hibiscus tea and let her fingers caress the jingles of nylon coin belts. The strange pulse of Arabic dance music played in most stalls, much nicer than England's dreary repetition of tinny *ho ho ho* tunes. Girls who walked past had gaudy scarves covering their hair, and even their faces. They stared at Amy in her black sweater and tartan micro mini. She stared right back. She was too shy to say hello, too awkward to pretend she hadn't heard them giggling.

Jason and Mazen were supposed to be escorting her, but she shook them off easily enough. It suited her to wander through all the colours and noise, not belonging, not caring. The boys eventually tracked her down in a jewellery stall cascading with silver, gold and turquoise beads.

'Don't buy here!' Mazen said earnestly. 'You buy from my brother's shop, very cheap, very nice.'

'Just looking,' she said.

That's how it felt, every day, wherever she went. Just looking. Cruising through, not part of a place, not settled.

'Are you homesick?' Jason asked suddenly.

She shook her head. Home was the last place she wanted to be – squashed into the four walls of the house with people talking at her, asking how she was, gushing over Claire's big baby bump.

'I'm not,' he boasted. 'I love it here. Much more fun than Crimbo at home. All my family ever do is memorize the TV guide, planning which dross to watch and arguing who gets to hold the remote.'

'I'm surprised you don't just put on reruns of *Action Archaeology!*'

'Oh my parents hate it. They're very, you know, shuffle along with life not drawing attention to yourself. They want me to be a dentist, or a solicitor. Something respectable. I had a real fight to come out here for the dig. Fortunately, I've saved up some cash from working weekends.'

'Don't you get paid for doing TV?' *Unlike me*, she thought.

'Yeah – that all goes into my university fund. They said I'll have to cough up for my own fees if I study Archaeology. Which, obviously I will. What about you?'

'What about me?'

'What d'you want to do?'

'Me? Nothing.' She didn't want to think about the past or the future. End of conversation.

Jason stared at her. 'Hedgehog,' he muttered. 'Come on, it's time to go.'

'Go where?'

'You'll see. It's my new second favourite place in the world.'

The sun was just setting as they reached the west bank of the Nile and approached the Windy Wadi. Work was done for the day. A strange light glowed over the east slope, where the excavations were. They approached the high fence surrounding the Cat Tomb. Jason knocked at the gate. Amy felt a shiver of apprehension. There was no sound beyond the fence until the gate slowly grated open and Farouk the overseer looked out. He was frowning. Amy shrank away. Then the frown vanished and Farouk laughed loudly. 'Welcome, welcome,' he said. He pulled the gate wide to let them through.

Oh.

Whatever Amy had expected beyond the fence, it wasn't this – this fairyland of light and sudden music.

'Happy Christmas! Surprise!' came voices from every direction. There was Dad, in his best *Slade on Tour* T-shirt, waving madly from behind a trestle table that was loaded with food and dotted with candles that burned in coloured glass cups. 'Here she is!' he bellowed. 'My little girl, who accidentally stumbled on this amazing site.'

Amy cringed as everyone grinned at her and clapped.

*Don't look at me.*

They'd all made an effort to be festive. Ellie wore the same T-shirt and combat trousers, but she had tinsel woven through her curls and glittery Santas bobbing from her ears. Rosa Hassan had swapped her lab coat for an embroidered galabeya tunic, while Kev and Dez had exchanged their camera equipment for cans of beer. Even Farouk's men were in a jolly mood. They had commandeered one corner of the compound, where they drank mint tea, smoked on a couple of hookah pipes and laughed at incomprehensible jokes. Dan the technician had set up a CD player with funky songs, though he still bopped along to his own headphones.

Jason grinned. 'They told me to keep you busy while they set this party up. Now come and have some grub. I'm starving.'

Amy let him dive into the refreshments. She followed slowly, edging round the inside of the fence. Watching everyone have fun was like seeing an episode of her life on TV. She didn't feel part of it.

The land within the fence had changed massively since she first lay amid the desert valley, feeling a chunk of limestone jostle her hand. Then, the newly-discovered doorway had been submerged in rocks and sand. Now, all that was cleared and broad steps led down into the ground. In place of a door there was a sturdy metal gate, fastened with a heavy-duty padlock. Anubis guarded the entrance. He looked up and yipped hello at Amy. She went to fuss him. He whined, trailed once round her boots then pressed his muzzle through the metal bars of the gate.

'You daft mutt, what's bugging you?'

Her dad came to join her, only just stopping himself

from ruffling her hair, which was braided in neat rows of red and black. 'All right, Munchkin? D'you like the party? Leave Anubis for now – I've got some things to show you first. Things from your tomb.'

She shivered. *My tomb*. She had a sudden picture of herself as a withered-up body hidden underground, surrounded by silence.

'You mean this place – the Cat Tomb?'

'Come and look . . .'

As part of the Christmas Eve celebrations certain objects from the new tomb had been set out in a quiet area, well away from the drink and the improvised dance floor, where Kev and Farouk were clapping and stamping to an Arabic beat. Ellie came over to help lift the objects from their nests of packing. She wore clean white gloves to handle them – no more casual groping around and grabbing. Amy was given a pair of gloves too. Her dad struggled to find a pair to fit his meaty hands.

'Here we go,' he said, popping something small in her palm.

'Cool! It's a wooden frog!'

'Found it on the floor of the antechamber, well, Ellie did. Got eyes like a hawk.'

'It's from an ancient Egyptian game called *senet*,' said Ellie. 'Put in the tomb to stop the dead person getting

197

bored in the afterlife. Unfortunately, there was one of the pieces missing – a hedgehog – and no bloody rules either. We haven't got a clue how to play it properly.'

'We've got a Monopoly game like that at home,' Amy laughed. 'It drives me crazy, not knowing how much money you're supposed to start with. Dad always makes the rules up.'

'Never mind that,' he snapped. 'How about this!'

He set a wooden case on the table. It was shaped like a cat looking forward and sitting on its back legs. A gap divided the case into two halves. There were still traces of grey and white paint in the grooves of the wood. Her dad showed off a fine silver necklace that had been found around the casket neck.

'We did a lovely sequence of filming yesterday, with Jason cracking this beauty open. I told him to keep it secret – wanted to show you myself. See, the casket splits and inside there's a mummy! A cat mummy! All wrapped up in sacking, poor thing. I thought you'd like it. Didn't you used to have a cat?'

'I still do. He's called Fat Lad.'

Ellie swallowed a smile. 'This one's called *Ta Miu*,' she said. 'It means Lady Cat.'

Amy stroked the head of the wooden case. 'Cats must be special in ancient Egypt, to get their own mummies.'

'Oh yes,' said her dad enthusiastically. 'Worshipped in some places – there's a city called Bubastis where they found thousands of cat mummies. The god Ra is said to take the form of a tom cat. Of course, this one was probably a pet belonging to the chap in the tomb.'

'*If* it was a bloke,' Ellie objected.

'Of course it's a man! You've seen the picture – it's definitely a man.'

'I'm not so sure . . .'

They became lost in a rehash of an old argument. Amy let them get on with it. She had found the final object, a white box decorated with brown and red stripes. The lid was loose. Peeping out was a row of identical turquoise figures, each with arms crossed and bodies wrapped in rows of hieroglyphic writing. Although they didn't have eyes painted on, they seemed poised on the brink of life, as if the right word would have them stretching out and moving.

'That's one of the *shabti* boxes,' said Ellie. 'There are still a couple left in the tomb.'

'Are they dolls?'

'Dolls? No! Shabtis are magical servants. They're brilliant! You get buried with a stack of these to do all the slogging in the afterlife. I mean, who feels like doing housework when they're dead? Or alive, for that matter.

Look, they're holding hoes, ready to work in the fields, and this criss-cross pattern on one shoulder represents a basket, for putting weeds or seeds in. Whatever needs doing in the afterlife, all you have to do is say, *Shabti, where are you?* and the shabti has to answer, *Here I am!* Wouldn't you just love a couple of your own?'

'It would revolutionize my homework situation,' Amy agreed. She regretted the comment as soon as she saw her dad's reaction.

'What's the matter with your homework?' he asked sharply. 'I heard your grades were going down the drain. You mother said . . .'

'It's fine!'

'Failing exams isn't fine. School told me you were letting things slide . . .'

'Dad!'

'I'm just saying . . .'

'Don't!'

He pulled his gloves off, glared and signalled for Ellie to pack things away.

'Kids!' he muttered. 'Think they know everything.'

Amy was resigned to the sudden crush of embarrassment. At least Ellie didn't give her the cold shoulder, and she didn't make things worse by spouting the equivalent of a patronizing pat on the head. She just closed the lid on the shabti box and said, 'These figures are the minions. There are also *reis* shabtis – overseers. They have fancy kilts and long whips. Your dad set one over the door inside the Cat Tomb, to make sure we're all working hard enough . . .'

Typical Dad joke.

'I only flunked one exam,' Amy said quietly. 'The Music teacher's rubbish anyway.'

'Mine was too. I wouldn't worry, as long as you pass History, of course.'

'I love History! I mean, I like it better than some other subjects . . .'

'Yeah? I thought you knew a bit about Egyptians already.'

'Not much. We don't do them much at school, I just, you know, read a bit about them.'

Ellie nodded. 'If you want, I've got a book you can borrow. Jason said you liked pictures of Duat in the tombs of the Valley of the Kings. The *Book of the Dead*, or Am Duat, is all about how souls find their way through the underworld. It's a good translation and the illustrations are amazing. I'll dig it out for you.'

Jason had been talking about her?

Amy looked across the enclosure to where he sat with a group of young men, laughing and chatting as they smoked the light applewood of the hookah pipe. He happened to glance up at the same moment. She was surprised to see a more than festive shine in his eyes. Surprised and pleased.

The candles were burning very low indeed as Dr Tony Clayton clambered on to a sturdy box and waved for the music to stop.

'Right everybody, roll up, roll up! Christmas Eve midnight is almost upon us, and since we can't be in church singing carols, or scoffing mince pies in front of the telly, we're going to celebrate by a special visit to TT440 – the tomb that has made our dear TV producers very happy. For those of you who've worked in 440 and 439, I'd like to thank you on behalf of *Action Archaeology!* For those unlucky souls who've yet to see inside . . . your curiosity is about to be rewarded! Leave your drinks outside, tread carefully, and follow me into the past . . . !'

He shepherded his team to the barred gate and flourished the key to the padlock. Amy had been sleepy until that moment, quietly watching stars prickle the Egyptian sky and just as quietly ignoring her dad's cracks about her needing a bunch of mistletoe. Now she woke up completely. She had no pockets in her kilt but she held the limestone cat picture hidden inside her long sleeve. Finally, finally . . .

Ellie laughed at her own sudden hesitation and said, 'I know I've been in already, but it's quite intimidating to be here at night. If all our lights went out we'd be surrounded by a very wide darkness. Makes me glad I don't believe in the ancient gods . . . though whether they cease to exist just because they're not worshipped any more, that's another question.'

Almost everyone looked up at the night sky, at patterns of stars that hadn't changed since pharaohs last ruled the land.

'Less of the philosophizing,' said Amy's dad.

'And don't you dare start on about curses!' groaned Jason. 'Mazen's dying to spin me more tales about how the excavators at Tutankhamun's tomb all suffered horrible fates. I was laughing it off till he got to the bit about Howard Carter's pet canary getting swallowed by a *snake*.'

Mazen nodded wisely. '*Naja haje.*'

Jason grimaced. 'And I'd rather have curses than cobras.'

Amy bit her lip. She didn't know if she was superstitious or not. She did hate the feeling she got seeing the eyes of the gods painted in the tombs in the Valley of the Kings, as if they were seeing into her heart and judging her.

'I don't believe in curses,' Rosa said, predictably enough.

'That's right,' agreed Amy's dad. 'We're all men of science here! And, er, women of science. Come on, Amy, you're looking a bit pale. Ignore all this doom and gloom rubbish! Don't listen to these old women, I mean – sorry, Rosa – paranoid freaks. Watch your step and in you go. Good job you're wrapped up warm,' he added. 'Gets chilly at night, doesn't it? Hey, isn't that Owen's jumper you're wearing . . .?'

Amy pretended not to hear him. She wanted to see the pictures. She wanted to see the cat with the glittering eyes.

# 19 Besieged!

*Save me from that god who steals souls,*
*who laps up corruption, who lives on what is putrid,*
*who is in charge of darkness,*
*who is immersed in gloom . . .*

(*Book of the Dead*)

There was only one way to run – away from the advancing army and into the safety of Anhai's garden.

Shabti wished he had his lightning-fast war chariot. He could have plunged, full of glory, straight into the heart of Deshret, instead of sprinting in the opposite direction, on foot like a commoner. But this was no coward's rout, it was a deliberate retreat. He knew that the walls of Kemet's compound weren't high enough to halt the enemy, while the walls around the white house would be easier to defend.

He called out as he ran, gasping, 'To the house, to the house!'

Keben, Reniseb and other overseers did their best to herd terrified animals into the garden. Supplies were hastily gathered up . . . or knocked over in the scramble for safety. Rip and Bite belted through the wooden gates, biting at the heels of workers who were slow. Soon Shabti stood in the open gateway with a jumbled crowd of animals and servants amongst the trees behind him. On and on the enemy came. They filled the air with their jabbering cries and stabbing spears. Just as the gates were being swung shut, a goat gone silly with fear bolted loose from the garden, straight under the archway and into the compound. Without thinking, Shabti ran after it. He grabbed the woven rope around its neck, meaning to drag it back to safety. The goat dug its heels into the ground. Shabti tugged and tugged on the halter.

A ring of fire rose up around the compound and smoky monsters were pouring through. The wretched goat just wouldn't move.

Hob shouted, 'Boy! Get back in here! We can't wait. You workers, close the gate . . . slide the bolt across!'

Anhai's house was sealed in. Shabti was trapped outside.

A fiery hand came sweeping through the air, bristling with claws. It tore the goat from his grasp, and flung the poor creature into a wide inferno of a mouth. Shabti gagged at the stench of burning meat. He was already on the run once more, flat at the gates, leaping like a monkey, hauling himself over . . . helped to the other side by Hob's brawny arms.

Sweet-scented sanctuary. Flower petals wafted loose as workers and livestock brushed past them. Fruit fell uneaten and was trampled to pulp. One pair of ducks was already swimming in the pond. The others had flown away, or been killed.

'The walls will hold them for a while,' Shabti panted. 'But not for ever. And we're trapped in here for now.' He looked around at the garden, then at the serene façade of the white house entrance. What weapons could they possibly use to fight monsters of dust and flame?

Dust and flame. Drought and fire.

His gaze turned to the ornamental pond in the centre of the garden. What would fight drought and fire? Water of course! That was why the monsters had dammed the river rather than swim across! Wind, too, could maybe blow them away . . . Quickly he told Hob his ideas.

'Water? Wind? Why should they work?'

'What do we have to lose by trying? Tell all the

workers to empty the pond and drain the water tanks. Pour *beer* on the creatures if you have to. We can climb on the garden walls and drown anything that comes close.'

'You're crazy.' Hob hesitated too long. He felt something tugging at the hem of his kilt. It was King, the big tawny cat, scratching and mewing. 'Now *I'm* crazy. Damn cat seems to think I should do something.'

Once his whip was in action the workers quickly did Hob's bidding. Shabti prowled from one corner of the garden to another, always with half an eye on the invisible spot that led out of Kemet down into the secret chamber . . .

Every kind of vessel was filled with water, although there were few at hand, since the house had more or less been stripped of objects. Workers monkeyed up the vines on the garden wall, or climbed on to the shoulders of their companions. Shabti lined his own shabby reed basket with large plant leaves, then filled it with pond water. Greatly to Keben's disgust, he scrambled up the man like a ladder, and crouched on the top of the wall.

He was scared and exhilarated at the same time. Where were the monsters? Would they come and show themselves? Yes! There were the tell-tale dust demons, rising up and drifting closer to the garden walls.

Smoky fires fed them. Now they looked almost solid. They were certainly hideous – every kind of mismatched animal deformity.

'Come on, you blistering fiends, coward demons . . . ! Come right to the wall!'

With a wild whoop Shabti tossed his water into the air. Where the drops fell, creatures sizzled and steamed. One especially guttural howl was cut short.

'Ha! Got you! Everyone, pour all the water! Throw whatever you've got at them!' He stood up on the wall and danced in triumph. He felt so jubilant he could have hoisted up his kilt and peed on the deformed army! It was going to work! The water really would work

For a while it seemed as if the defences would hold and the siege be broken. Wave after wave of Chaos was wiped out by the water. Then the workers found they were scooping nothing but weeds and flapping fish out of the pond. Worse still, the two massive shapes Shabti had seen crossing the fire line during the first attack weren't so easily intimidated. The Serpent of Chaos thrived on destruction, whichever side suffered defeat. As for the other grotesquery, it moved slowly but steadily, as if it couldn't be halted, couldn't be killed; as if it would keep on hunting until the prey was caught and then . . .

Yellow eyes glittered and sharp teeth ground together in pink gums.

*Bam! Bam! Bam!*

The high garden gate shook as powerful forces pounded against it.

Shabti hid his fear and stood before the workers.

'We can't expect the gate to hold much longer. You lot, yes *you*, go brace yourself against it. The rest of you, find whatever weapons you can and form a line in front of the house. We'll fight them hand to hand.'

'We don't have weapons,' said one field worker. 'We dig and weed.'

Shabti brandished his hoe. 'I'll fight them with this if I have to. What have you got?'

'We collect the harvest,' said another worker. 'We haven't got hoes.'

'So use a sickle.'

Other workers sang out a chorus of objections.

'We work the *shaduf* . . .'

'We take the cattle out . . .'

'We herd the geese . . .'

'No!' Shabti cried. 'I already explained this – you all have to do *new* things now. Hob, tell them!' But even Hob's whip couldn't stop the workers breaking formation and moving about the garden, upset and uncertain.

*Bam! Bam! Bam!*

Suddenly, a new voice spread over the din of the siege. Shabti looked up to see Anhai standing fearlessly at the edge of the roof of the white house. Her braids were loose and her white dress was stained grey from the dust and shadows. Her hands were spread in the air before her, tracing invisible words that fell down from the stars. She called out over the wall.

'Fall! Crawl away, Apophis, you enemy of Ra! Go, be drowned in the lake of first-flowing water! Get back, you rebel, at the knives of Ra's light! You shall be decapitated with a knife, your face shall be cut away, your head shall be removed by him who rules this land, your bones shall be broken!'

Shabti was stunned. Too astonished to move. He'd never seen Anhai so animated, never known she had such a strength within her, or a knowledge of deep magic.

At first the snake recoiled at Anhai's challenge. Where it had been a dense mass of green, now its skin crumbled like the crest of a sand dune blown by the wind. Still it kept writhing around the wall. Its great body undulated inside the mud bricks and plaster, giving the wall a strange and obscene rippling effect. Anhai's spell was defiant but not destructive. As black smoke and wild fire choked the compound the snake grew in strength once more.

Anhai turned towards the garden, where frightened animals trampled her neat paths and exotic plants. None of the workers, save Hob, would see sense long enough to follow Shabti's hoarse orders.

*Bam! Bam! Bam!* went the battering at the gates.

'Servants! All you shabtis! There's work to be done. Where are you?'

As one the workers snapped to attention and turned to face their mistress. As one their chins went up. As one they called, 'HERE I AM!' Shabti was no exception. There was no time to wonder why Anhai had called them *all* shabtis, as if it wasn't his own special name.

She commanded, 'Take up tools or sticks. Do as the boy says. Face the gate and fight whatever comes through. Do it now!'

*Bam! Bam! Bam!*

Confusion was forgotten, aimlessness cast aside. Each worker began a diligent search for a possible weapon.

*Bam! Bam! Bam!*

The wooden gates could hold out no longer. They bowed, buckled and finally split open. The desert poured inside. Shabti raised his hoes and wished, not for the first time, that he had a company of Young Heroes standing with him in the last defence, ready to rout these hordes of sand and Chaos. There was no question of escaping, of saving himself. His one fierce thought was to do whatever it took to protect the proud lady of the white house.

Suddenly a breeze began to stir the leaves of the garden. At last! A long-hoped-for wind! The Deshret demons wavered as new gusts buffeted them in a steady rhythm. What was causing such a stir? Shabti looked up through the grit to see the most incredible sight of the evening. Anhai had vanished. In her place was the tall grey heron, stretched out fully, wide wings beating in the air. Each sweep of the heron's feathers sent a wind cascading over the garden, making monsters crumble and fall. Now Shabti wielded his hoe with savage delight. Hob bellowed and sent his whip curling, causing many a monster's ruin. Rip and Bite were rampaging in the thick of the fight and every worker fought with a steady loyalty more inspiring than the manic lunges of the desert army.

The taste of victory was sweet but fleeting.

Apophis the serpent scorned gateways. Thick with power and swollen with venom, it reared up over the stone pylons, right to the rooftop of the house itself. The heron didn't cower or falter. It would be defiant to the end . . . and the end looked close.

Forgetting everything else, Shabti clambered over the broken gates and fought to get close to the serpent's vast body. He raged at it, battering it over and over. His hoe could not cut the tough scales. The snake barely noticed him. High above, its mouth opened wide, showing every single wicked fang. It lunged for the heron.

That was when a cat leaped on to the roof. It was King, looking impossibly large now, more like a lion than a domestic tabby... more like a demon itself, with blades of obsidian, not a mere cat's claws. Spitting and hissing, fur bristling in spikes, King launched himself at the serpent's eyes.

*Stamp stamp stamp.*

Half hidden by the snake's bulk, the second nightmare predator approached. What was it pursuing so relentlessly?

*Me?* Shabti whipped round in time to feel the stench of carrion-breath on his face and the glare of devouring eyes burning deep into his heart. He backed away, stumbling over the gates once more, back, back into the garden, too terrified to fight, trembling so hard his bones almost shook loose. The creature pursued, slow but relentless. Shabti took one more step back, lost his balance, floundered and fell.

## 20 Dawn Chorus

*None are mighty in the night and none can stand alone*
*without a helper close beside.*

(The Instruction of King Amenemhat)

All night long Amy fought a battle between sleeping and waking nightmares. Her dreams were populated with all the strange pictures she had seen in the Cat Tomb, and images from the book Ellie had loaned her, the *Book of the Dead*. People in profile marched endlessly round her head, some in white kilts and jewelled collars, some carrying bushels and baskets, or leading cattle. A waterfall of hieroglyphs cascaded through moving colours – the green of trees, the white of a house, the red of the desert.

Too much!

She tried to wake up, but the room was thick with

darkness, and that was when she saw worse things, even with her eyes open. Memories spattered like rain. Even hiding behind her pillow she could still see a dead white face, shocking in the glare of steady headlights. She heard a phone ringing – always that bloody phone ringing! When she reached to answer it, the ringing stopped. No messages.

Her ribs ached, her leg ached, her head . . . her head was pounding!

She got out of bed and pulled on Owen's sweater. It was grubby and shapeless now and no longer smelled of him. No longer looked like the sort of thing he would have worn. Claire hadn't wanted her to keep it – said it should go to the charity shop, along with the rest of Owen's gear. Probably didn't want Amy to hold on to anything of his, except the enduring memory of his body crumpled in a wrecked car.

Amy pulled the curtains open. Wouldn't cry. Couldn't cry. At Owen's funeral everyone said, 'Isn't she taking it well? Hasn't she made a quick recovery?' Amy pulled away from any suspicion of sympathy. She didn't want it. Didn't deserve it. Claire's face had been a permanent blotch of tears.

Now what?

Dawn was only just grazing the skyline of the hotel

garden. Hidden in the palm trees and shrubs, birds didn't just twitter sweetly, they practically screeched their welcome to the new day. *Chorus* couldn't describe the noise – cacophony was more like it.

The *Action Archaeology!* team were having a slightly later start than usual. They were all sleeping off the fun of Christmas Day – the crazy banquet of food served on the hotel terrace, silly party games, presents, bottle after bottle of sparkling wine, beer and champagne. With mobile service still intermittent, Amy had managed a crackly phone conversation with her mum, who sounded as if she were talking with her head in a bucket, the line was so bad.

'Everything all right?' Mum asked. 'Are you enjoying yourself?'

'Yeah. Everything's fine.'

'Have you found any treasure yet? Dad says filming's going well.'

Treasure? Amy was still reeling from the experience of her midnight visit to the Cat Tomb. She couldn't believe such beautiful objects and artworks had all been waiting underground for her accidental discovery. She was also uncomfortable with the fact that everything in the antechamber of TT440 had been painted there or placed there only for the benefit of the dead person. What did it matter to a corpse? Ellie said the pictures and objects represented abundance in the afterlife. Amy didn't like the idea that death wasn't the end, nor the ancient Egyptian belief that dead spirits could return to the land of the living to torment and haunt anyone who'd offended them.

'Hello? Hello?' came her mum's woolly voice. 'Sorry, love, I can't hear you. I said, did you find any treasure? Cleopatra's tomb, maybe?'

'I went in the new tomb,' Amy said. 'It's not royal though. Dad says it belonged to this Egyptian man painted on the wall, but Ellie Powell, she's this student archaeologist, she reckons the tomb got used by someone else, maybe a girl, if it was needed in a hurry.'

'That's nice. You're not eating uncooked fruit or salads, are you? Remember what I said about getting a poorly tummy.'

'Well, it's not exactly roast beef and Yorkshire pudding for Christmas dinner out here, Mum.'

Much to Ellie's disappointment.

'Of course not. We've got Grandma Clayton round for lunch. She says thank you for her present, though I'm afraid the dogs ate most of the chocolates, and she's sorry not to see you.'

The feeling wasn't mutual.

'Is . . . is Claire there?'

'Oh, sorry, dear. Your sister's out walking Grandma's dogs. She'll call you when she gets back, don't worry.'

Sure. Just like she'd called every other day. Not.

Mum signed off. 'Take care and have a lovely holiday. Love you lots, happy Christmas!'

Happy Christmas, happy Boxing Day, happy New Year.

People were always expecting everyone to be *happy*.

And she wasn't.

She crept through the quiet hotel corridors and slipped out on to the riverside terrace. It was dotted with wooden tables and pale yellow sunshades. Right at the water's edge there were chairs facing the Nile. She chose one and huddled into it, keeping her hands inside the jumper sleeves. It was cold before the sun rose fully. She half wondered if it would be nice to be nestling in someone's warm arms, feeling his breath on her neck and maybe his lips softly kissing . . .

A red gash split the far horizon, like a belly split open in battle. Soon the dawn chorus was mingled with the echoing call to prayer. Little boats tooled up and down the river, neatly dodging the great cruise ship leviathans that were making an early start. Beyond them a line of palm tree silhouettes marked the west bank. The cliffs were dark, waiting for Ra's light to turn the desert rocks pink then orange then sandy red. They were so plain, so barren, it was strange to think that their rocks hid tombs so filled with colour and life . . . as well as the still bodies of the dead.

Her dad had pointed out the door to the burial chamber in the Cat Tomb. A wooden measuring rod was placed before it, to give scale in the photographs.

'That's where we'll find the body,' he said. 'The door's intact, still got the rope knots across to seal it. It means robbers never found this place, and whatever's inside has been untouched for centuries.'

'Should you open the door?' she asked. 'Aren't they supposed to rest in peace?'

'Oh, we won't disturb him too much.'

'Her,' said Ellie.

'*Him.*'

'Her!'

'For god's sake Ellie, there's a painting of a man with his family on the wall right behind you, of course it'll be a *him* in the coffin.'

'And his name's been scratched off the walls because someone else needed the tomb. It's not unheard of.'

'As if this rich bloke would let someone else use his tomb. These places cost a fortune to build.'

'He would if it was someone in his family. One of his

daughters. There are two shown in the family group.'

Amy had looked at the scene in the antechamber, showing a serene Egyptian man seated on an ebony chair, with a woman beside him – improbably smaller – and three white-clad children. She hadn't really bothered about him much, although she noticed the man's belly rippled a bit, reminding her of her dad. She'd been more amused by a pet monkey climbing up the back of the chair. The cat on the riverbank, that was still her favourite painting of all. On Christmas Eve she'd blanked out arguments over who was buried in the tomb, and let her eyes fill with the shining gold of the cat's eyes.

*Stay here a while*, the gaze seemed to say.

'Right, everyone out!' said her dad. 'Back on Boxing Day!'


And so Boxing Day dawned. The river turned from red-black to blue as the light grew brighter.

Amy took a deep breath and one final look at the cliffs before creeping back to her bed for an extra hour of sleep and dreams. Although the Christmas Eve visit to TT440 had been a bit of an anticlimax, she had a feeling squirming inside, a sense that something was going to *happen* and she didn't want that. She just wanted everything to go tootling along safe and normal. Still, at least she was part of the day's plans, even if her inclusion was a bit of an afterthought, when her dad realized there'd be no one left to baby-sit her. While Dad, Jason and Kev took to the skies in a helicopter for some dramatic aerial views of the wadi, she and Ellie were given the job of sieving through the sand on the floor of the Cat Tomb, searching for tiny artefacts and lost fragments. Rather like Cinderella, really, sorting peas and beans for the stepmother, while the stepsisters got to go to the ball.

Then, and only then, would the team film the next big scene, the breakthrough into the silent burial chamber of the Cat Tomb. Last resting place of the unknown owner.

# 21 The Quiet Room

*One fancies thee sighing forlorn through these*
*desolate halls when all is silent and the moon*
*shines down the valley.*
(Amelia B. Edwards, *A Thousand Miles Up the Nile*)

A tower of silver boxes broke his fall, and almost his back. Shabti lay across them like a rag doll. He waited to be seized by reptilian teeth and devoured. For a moment or an eternity – he couldn't tell which – he stared into darkness and heard only silence. Where had the Chaos gone? The noise? The ravenous beasts of Deshret? Slowly he became aware of his surroundings and realized what had happened. Escaping from the deformed monster, he'd fallen through the invisible hole and into the strange underground room.

He jolted alert and promptly fell off the boxes on to

the sandy floor, cracking his shins against unseen shapes. Warily he held his arms out and felt around, wishing he had a lamp. As his eyes became used to the gloom, he noticed that the darkness wasn't complete. His lungs flowered with the freshness of clear air and he practically ran towards the pale rose hue of early morning. The way out was blocked by rigid metal bars – no freedom that way. Suddenly furious, he shook the gate and battered at the lock with his wooden hoe.

He felt like an animal in a cage, waiting to be butchered. At any moment he expected ravening monsters to tear at the invisible hole and come tumbling into the underground room, all arms, legs, teeth and claws.

Well he wouldn't wait! There had to be some way out of this underground prison.

Flakes of paint fell from the walls as he felt his way round the room, probing for other doors or windows. Something glittered. He stopped. Two eyes were shining. A monster? No, a cat, painted on the far wall, holding a wicked knife in one front paw and a writhing serpent under the other. The cat's eyes were round and golden with an illuminating glow. The cat itself was sitting on a riverbank, surrounded by a vivid riot of animals, plants and fish. He saw darting dragonflies, waving papyrus fronds and fat fish swimming in ripples of blue. Countless birds filled the painted sky, so lifelike he half-expected them to shake their feathers and fly out of the picture.

Then he noticed the other walls, also covered in colours. People sat on one side, eyes gazing into eternity. On another wall he saw Anhai's white house with a tree-clustered garden and fields of crops growing as high as a man's shoulder.

Anhai.

The battle.

Should he go back?

The tawny cat's gaze held him again. Those glittering golden eyes looked beyond him to a plain, square area on another wall. A strange stick was set on the floor before this wall. It was striped red and white, with black shapes painted on.

Why would the cat look at the wall?

He glanced back at the ceiling. Somewhere beyond the invisible hole Anhai's lovely home was being battered relentlessly. This was no time to stand and wonder about things. King had helped him this far, perhaps he could be trusted further. Shabti gripped his hoe. Tiredness and fear were forgotten. *Smash!* He cracked the first layer of plain plaster. Behind it were small stones packed together tightly – there *was* a second doorway on this wall. All he had to do was batter his way through and then . . .

Then what?

He pulled rocks and plaster chunks aside. Darkness flowed out but the cat's eyes kept shining and as soon as the gap was big enough he dropped his hoe and clambered through.

It was another room, smaller than the first. Closed in. Claustrophobic. Again his fingertips did the searching. They spread through the empty air and went roving across naked walls. When he took a few tentative steps they grazed the smooth surface of something in the centre of the room. A box.

Silence pressed down on him. The air was hot but he felt cold as he touched the object. His fear grew. The box was large enough and long enough to hold a human body. With his heart beating far too fast, he traced the shape of shoulders and the stylized bumps of a human face. A mass of leaves crumbled under his touch, filling the darkness with a sudden scent of jasmine and other pretty perfumes. He jumped back.

*Anhai!*

He knew the smell – had breathed it in every moment spent in her house. What did this box have to do with her?

Nestling amongst the dried flowers was a harder object. His hands recognized the shape. Even though he couldn't see the glittering colours he knew, without any doubt, that it was the same as the jewelled eye Anhai wore around her neck – the symbol of the wedjat.

*I don't understand! Don't want to understand!*

Slowly he backed away from the box. A nasty lump of guilt began to crawl up his throat, making breathing difficult and thinking almost impossible. Colours and shapes collided in his mind . . . the blue of a wide sky, the red of high cliffs. A road, sandy yellow. Clouds of dust. Horses pounding, greyhounds racing, people dancing, banners waving. And a box, just like this box, laden with fresh-cut flowers and painted with eyes that looked up at the all-seeing sun.

Pain crushed his skull. He gasped and staggered. This was no time to be ill! No time to be dragged back into memories! Suddenly he saw the white gleam of sharp teeth and the glare of malevolent eyes. There it was, drawn on the wall above the box, the very creature that had been pursuing him! The picture grinned.

He fled. Ran back to the gate. Shook it some more. Shouted for help. Was there an answer? He paused. Listened. Was someone actually coming to open the gate? Could he actually run free once more?

Thoughts of Anhai and the battle in Kemet tugged at his jubilation.

*Forget them!* screamed one voice in his head. *Save yourself!*

Footsteps crunched on the rocky ground beyond the gate.

Balanced on the brink of freedom Shabti felt a curious sense of certainty settle around him, like a warm fur cloak.

*Yes*, he thought, *I* will *save myself, and I'll hack down anything that tries to stop me!*

## 22 Fifteen Minutes

*. . . the larger valleys suddenly became seething rivers . . .*

(Letter from Howard Carter to his mother,

October 1918)

'Not a cloud in sight!' her dad declared, as he pulled on his best explorer jacket and Indiana Jones hat. 'A perfect day for filming.'

Kev didn't look convinced. 'Weather report says some clouds possible, westwards, over the plateau.'

'Miles away! Nothing to bother us. Right then, chaps, tally ho and chocks away! Wave if you see us flying over, Amy!' And off the boys went to play in a helicopter.

Ellie was fairly jolly company until they got to the Windy Wadi and met Farouk. His face was grave and there were dark rings around his eyes.

He asked Ellie, 'Dr Clayton will be away today, yes?'

'Yep. A helicopter flight to film the site from above, then some big meeting about the Cat Tomb here. The Supreme Council of Antiquities are getting very excited about this place.'

He nodded. 'I am afraid they are not the only ones.'

'Have people been getting nosey? Asking questions? We've been lucky to get away with secrecy for so long. Bloody treasure-hunters.'

Farouk shrugged. 'People come. People go. They see boxes. Fences. The metal gate. They wonder.'

'It's only a matter of time before some journalist gets hold of the story then the whole world will be camping out here wanting a piece of the action . . . or the goodies.' She paused. 'Is there something else the matter?'

'Perhaps yes, perhaps no.'

'Come on, Farouk, you're the best work boss on the west bank, everyone says so. We trust you. Tell me what's bothering you.'

Amy hung back politely . . . not so far off she couldn't hear the overseer's voice when he next spoke.

'I watched last night, alone in the wadi. At the end of the night I hear, how do you say, *noises*? I looked inside but there was no one there. See, the gate is locked. I have the key safe. The gate did not open. No one went in. No one came out. This dog and I are certain. But the noises under the ground at dawn . . . we are not happy about that.'

He rested one hand on Anubis's glossy black head. The dog was strangely subdued, although every once in a while he lifted his wet nose and sniffed the still air.

Amy looked around to try and guess what he was sensing. As far as she could tell, the wadi looked the same as always. Cliffs, rocks, sky, sun, clouds. OK, the clouds were new, but they were high up and far away, just dainty white wisps.

From the wadi she couldn't see the thicker clouds out in the desert highlands. They were heavy with rain.

Ellie said, 'We'll be in the tomb most of the morning, so we can keep an ear out for anything odd. We're sieving sand for small finds. Mazen's welcome to help too.'

Mazen shook his head. 'Me and Anubis, we guard you.' He too looked around the wadi, as if expecting terrorists or tomb robbers to leap out of every crevasse.

'My men have a holiday, but I will be here all day,' said Farouk. 'You will be safe.'

Ellie laughed. 'We'll be fine. Lock the fence, but leave the tomb chamber gate open, please.'

Farouk switched on the electric generator so they'd have power in the tomb, then undid the padlock on the corrugated fence and pushed the metal sheet open far enough to let them squeeze through. He took another set of keys and unlocked the bolt on the strong metal gate that had been set across the original doorway. 'I will bring mint tea soon,' he said.

'Cheers, Farouk. See you in a bit.'

The lights went on. Ellie shook her head to see an untidy pile of silver boxes. 'Typical! Kev and Dez have left loads of their camera kit here. Guess we'll work round them, Ames. God knows enough people have tramped through here, but if we start sieving near the door we should— *Good God!* Look at that!'.

Amy trembled when she saw what Ellie was pointing at. On Christmas Eve the plastered-over doorway in the far wall of the antechamber had been whole and sealed with intricate knots. Now there was a ragged hole and a pile of plaster and rubble.

'No wonder Farouk heard noises,' Ellie said grimly. 'Someone's definitely tried breaking in. I hope they didn't get away with anything.'

'It could have been Dad.'

'What, when he cloned himself on Christmas Day and nipped over in between drinks? Sorry, Amy, that was snappy. Only this is bad. This is really bad. Even your dad wouldn't do something this monumental, especially if Kev wasn't here to film it, and he would never breach the wall in such a rough and crappy way. This is a complete mess.'

'Farouk said the gate was locked.'

'It couldn't have been.'

'Shall I go get him?'

'No! I want to think about this before I get Farouk involved . . .'

Ellie took out her camera and began to record the damage. Just as she focused for a shot of the floor she saw something small and darted forward to pick it up.

'Wooden splinters? Where'd these come from?'

'I guess there is another room after all,' Amy said nervously.

'Oh yes, we knew there would be. The antechamber is always linked to a burial chamber, which must be what the robbers were after. The treasures inside the sarcophagus itself. Amy, look in here! It's just alive with colour!'

Ellie shone her torch through the doorway. The ceiling of the tiny room within was a galaxy of stars and every part of every wall had been plastered and painted, right into the shadow of each corner. The floor was bare and rough, but that hardly mattered, since most of it was covered with a large human-shaped coffin.

Unlike the cracked stone sarcophagus of the chariot,

this one was made of painted wood and immaculate. The entire surface of the coffin was crammed with exquisite and intricate designs, painted in colours that shone as brightly as if they were freshly put on that morning – reds, whites, black, blues, greens and yellows. Goddesses stretched out wings with countless feathers. Geometric patterns jostled for space with mysterious symbols. Gold leaf shimmered in the first light to break the darkness in centuries.

Most haunting of all was the face on the coffin. It was a three-dimensional design of flawless beauty, the smooth face of a young girl with almond-shaped eyes and a serene mouth that almost smiled.

Hieroglyphs streamed down the walls, in between scene after scene that could have been drawn straight from Ellie's copy of the *Book of the Dead*.

Ellie squinted and tried to make sense of them. 'Some of these are familiar,' she said. 'I think I can get the gist. Being a geeky Egyptologist finally pays off! Hang on, I'll paraphrase what I think this bit says . . . "Only a child, the afraid, no *frightening* dark swallowed. I am young . . . something something . . . I am a young girl without fault." I was right, it is a girl's tomb. That's the girl's name, right there. Anhai.'

*Anhai.*

Amy was awed at the fact they'd found a name. She got her phone out to grab a quick photo of the beautiful grey heron painted above the coffin.

Ellie quickly took some more pictures, even though she didn't want to use the flash too often. 'Right, that'll do. Whatever the robbers came for, they obviously didn't find it, because the coffin's still sealed. We'd best go see if we can get a message to your dad. He'll have a heart attack when he sees what's happened.'

She turned to clamber through the gouged-out doorway.

'Can you hear that?' Amy asked suddenly.

Ellie paused. 'Hear what?'

'A sort of rumbling . . .'

She got no further. What happened next was so entirely unexpected, so utterly impossible, they were both too stunned to move . . . even if there had been any way of escaping. The lights fused, the noise grew deafening and the underground tomb was suddenly invaded by a high wave of stones, sludge and water that pummelled into Ellie and swept her right into the burial chamber, tossing her against the wall. Amy was battered by water-borne rocks. Twice she was lost in the swirling murk, twice she surged upwards to scream, or breathe, or choke. On the third time she lost her footing completely, slipped under the water and was gone.

Fifteen minutes. That's how long it had taken for a sudden rainstorm on the desert plateau to grow into a devastating flood that tore up desert rocks, ran into every cliff fissure and flattened the fences of the Windy Wadi.

# 23 Desolation

*Round the decay*
*Of that colossal wreck, boundless and bare*
*The lone and level sands stretch far away.*

(Percy Bysshe Shelley, Ozymandias)

*I* will *save myself*, Shabti thought, *but I will save Lady Anhai too.*

He climbed up the boxes and used every last spurt of strength to heave himself upwards.

His eyes prickled. What could he see?

It wasn't darkness; it wasn't light either.

If it had been night, a banner of stars would have spread overhead, unmoving and ageless. If day, the sun would have burned away the shadows. When he emerged into Kemet both night and day had vanished, leaving a stain of red so malevolent it glowered in a parody of light.

He climbed slowly out of the hole. His lungs rasped as he breathed the red air in. The whole of Kemet was smothered in sand. No, not sand. As he took a few tentative steps, clouds of cloying red ash rose wearily around his feet and ankles.

Kemet had burned.

No battle raged now. There was no sign of life anywhere. No sound. Everything was dead or deadened by the ash. Fine flakes of it still wafted in the air, gritting his mouth and making his eyes sting. In a daze he wandered across the garden. The stone pylon was cracked. The wooden lotus gates were twisted on their hinges. They had been hacked by some obscene weapon and smeared with dark streaks.

'Hello?'

As in a nightmare, when he opened his mouth to shout only a weak whisper crawled from his lips and dropped slowly to the floor.

No reply. No movement. No life.

That pile of rusty-red rubble, was that where the Night House had been? That trough, wasn't that where cows had lapped water? Those charred sticks, hadn't they once been looms, where bright cloths were woven? Had those crumpled vats once frothed with beer? Had these baskets once been whole and fruit-full?

Further and further he drifted into the ashen ruins.

'Is anyone here?'

No one. No workers, no monsters.

He wandered across an expanse of ash that had once been a barley field. The very place he'd first woken with his hoe. He came to where the river used to flow. Now it was nothing but a channel of cracked red mud, speckled with the tiny skeletons of scorched fish. Not so far along, the massive carcass of Lady Hippo had been stripped bare. The bones were red too.

*I could keep walking for ever*, he thought. *Walk across the desert, climb the mountains, keep going till I crumble to red sand myself . . .*

There he stood, one thin, lost boy in a wasteland.

Something grey wafted past his eyes even though there was no breeze to blow it. One feather. Almost all that was left of a land once teeming with life.

The feather tickled a memory – something he was meant to do – somewhere he was meant to be. Of course! The grey heron! The white house.

Back he ran, wading through the desolation.

'Lady Anhai!'

He cursed himself for falling out of the garden, for staying so long in the underground chamber. Guilt made his legs heavy but still he ran. He burst through the door of the house and skidded from one empty room to another. He called her name over and over. Got no reply. Came to a stop in the hall of beautiful columns, now bare of all luxuries. Without the light of the sun or Anhai's alabaster lamps it was very dark. In one corner of the hall a shadow the colour of old blood shifted. It began to move closer. Was it the hideous monster that had followed him from Deshret? Was this how it would end – being attacked and devoured? Alone and unremembered?

Shabti backed away but there was nothing left to hide behind. The only weapon he had was his hoe – just a stupid wooden weeding tool! What could he do against forces that had destroyed so much so swiftly?

'Come out and fight in the light!' he shouted with more courage than he felt.

'Light?' growled the shadow's voice. 'You call *this* light? This pestilential muck?'

'. . . Hob?'

'That's *Master Hob* to you, boy.' The shadow stepped forward. His fine kilt was torn and bloodless claw marks were gouged into his skin.

'What . . . what happened, Master?'

'After you *ran away*, you mean?'

'I didn't! I fell! There was . . . never mind. I came back.'

'Not much to come back to, is there, boy? Crops in cinders. Animals burned. Workers crushed to powder. When I feared Deshret's coming I never knew there was *so much* to fear. The balance is lost, chaos overwhelms us.'

Hob sagged – no longer a bullying overseer but bent like a tired old man. Shabti looked around for a chair. There were none. No furniture of any kind.

'Here, hold my shoulder and lean for a bit. Ow! The other one, please. This one's sore.'

'Ay, you came back, boy, and I'm glad of that at least. You missed a rare sight, I tell you.'

'I saw King fight that Chaos snake, Apophis. I saw the grey heron beating off the storm. It looked as if our defences would hold.'

'They did – I'll give you that – as long as anything *could* stand against the battering of abominations. I might've been proud of your fine strategies if there'd been time to waste on that sort of feeling.' Hob hawked and spat out a grey-flecked gobbet of saliva. 'Sprayed 'em good and proper, we did, making 'em smoke black when the water hit 'em. Shrieks? I never heard a sound like it. Music to my ears, it was. Pure music. This mess is going to take a long time to clear up, mind. A long, long time. Lots of hard back-breaking work for you, my lad . . .'

'What about the snake? What about King?'

'Ah, that I don't know. Had troubles of my own. Apophis is gone for now. The cat too, as far as I can see. The balance is back again. Nothing here, though. Nothing left. Nothing. They got my pups!' he mourned. 'My own bad brutes!'

'Rip and Bite are dead?'

'Not without a fight! Rip got this griffin – cackling misbegotten thing with wings, never seen the like. Good old Rip leaped up and tore its stinking throat out. Never knew a dog so fierce. One yelp, that's all I heard as the talons got him. And Bite . . . let's just say that whatever sort of creature it was swallowed Bite down whole, it didn't live to digest him.'

This was awful. Shabti was amazed how upset he was to hear the two dogs were dead. Thinking of death . . .

'Did he . . . did he get the monster with lion's hair and crocodile teeth?'

This was the nightmare that had been following him so relentlessly.

'Lion's hair? No. It was more like a scorpion than anything else. Well at least Rip and Bite died defending my lady and that's all any of us should hope for.'

'Lady Anhai, is she . . . ?'

Hob didn't speak. He pointed silently to a set of stairs leading upwards.

She was on the roof still. Not so proud as before, more grey and insubstantial. She barely noticed his arrival.

'No where to fly to now,' she said sadly. 'I'm all broken.'

'Can you walk?' Shabti asked.

She shrank back. 'Get away from me!'

'I'm not the enemy! Come on! Things may be quiet but we don't know if it's safe yet.'

Menace still made the air heavy. Out in the compound, something that wasn't a simple breeze made the ash ripple.

Anhai was genuinely too weak to walk, but not so feeble she couldn't protest at Shabti hoisting her into his arms.

'You're a dirty dungball!'

'Exactly. I'm a common little servant boy who can beat you at senet any day.'

'Cannot!'

'Can!'

'Not!'

'Can.'

'You don't know anything – not even your own name! Silly boy! Silly shabti! There's work to do, where are you, shabti?'

'Here I am!' he replied immediately.

That made her laugh, but it wasn't a merry sound.

Arguing like this he got her down from the roof. She was so light – light as a feather! The only heavy thing about her was the jewelled eye hanging round her neck. When he looked at the eye his mind said one word – *whole*. Somehow he had to make Anhai whole again.

Her skin was softer than ash. He hadn't imagined how lovely that would feel against his scabs, scars and calluses.

When he saw his mistress, Hob's voice was rough with emotion. 'There's something wrong with her. She wouldn't come down with me. Says something's snapped and she's lost her way.'

'Lost her mind,' said Shabti impatiently. 'Look, I think I know a place I can take her, away from here.'

'Where you hid before?'

'I didn't mean to hide! A monster got so close I couldn't fight it. The one with the crocodile mouth and the lion's mane.'

There was a long pause before Hob spoke again. 'Well, I do believe there could be some things no man can fight, nor boy neither. If you've got a demon like that after you, there's no weapon I know of can hold it back. Now then, my lady, you're to go with your servant here.'

'He's not *my* shabti!' Anhai snapped. 'He's a whirlwind, an earthquake, a lightning bolt that splits you in two!'

*Delirious*, thought Shabti, although Anhai obviously believed what she was saying, even if no one else understood her.

Once again the ashes all round stirred as if moved by the breath of some vast creature.

Hob knelt down and kissed Anhai's hand tenderly. 'Goodbye, my lady,' he said, with as much courtesy as any nobleman. To Shabti he said, 'Make her safe, boy, or you'll have *me* on your back, and I'm worse than any of Deshret's spawn, understand?'

Understand? Shabti understood nothing more than the urge to get Anhai away before any monsters crawled back to claim them.

'Aren't you coming with us?' he asked Hob. 'There's room. A way out. You could take care of Anhai yourself. Not have to rely on me. Look, this twist of fur, it's the rope I used to climb down. It's fine but it's strong enough to hold your weight.'

'You saying I'm *fat*, boy? You won't catch me crawling through any unnatural *hole*, and yes, I know your secrets, you worm! I watched you wiggle out of it – out of nowhere it looked to me. Take my lady and keep her safe till I see what can be salvaged of this place.'

'Kemet's in ruins! Look, even the white house is starting to crack and collapse.'

'Then I'll build it again.'

'Out of what?'

'Ashes, if I have to, to keep her cool and shaded.'

Hob simply couldn't let go of his role as overseer of Anhai's estate.

Her soft voice calmed him.

'The balance is broken, Hob. Things have to be made right again – made whole. There won't be any house or garden any more.'

These words actually made sense to Shabti, though he couldn't have said why. However, they were forgotten as the air was split with a cry as cruel as a crocodile bite.

Quickly Hob said, 'Enough of that, my lady. Let the boy go first and I'll pass you down. Be speedy now. This ash, it's getting thicker . . . like mud . . . like ruddy *quicksand*.'

Shabti had already wiggled into the invisible hole and lowered himself through. He reached up for Anhai. She was looking over Hob's shoulder. Her mouth was open in a silent scream. It was the first time Shabti had ever seen her properly scared.

'I know that creature,' she shouted out. 'I've seen it before! Head of a crocodile, mane of a lion, lion's paws and hippo legs . . .'

Shabti was nearly sick at the description. The very same monster that had so nearly caught him during the battle! It was coming back again!

Without another word, Hob let Anhai fall through the hole. As she tumbled down the fur string strained, stretched . . . and snapped. Shabti looked up to see Hob's head and mad hair silhouetted against the red sky beyond.

'Jump!' he yelled. 'Jump now!'

With a shrug and a farewell salute, Hob turned his back on the hole and faced the thing that made the ground shake as it stamped ever nearer.

He taunted, 'Over here, carrion breath! Come see how you like the feel of my whip on your skin! Yah! Gnash your crocodile teeth all you like. Shake your mane! Show me your brawn! Bring your fight to someone worthy of it!'

Once, twice, three times the whip cracked, then all sounds of Kemet faded away and the hole closed for ever.

# 24 Catastrophe

*The Nile is long and life is short.*
(Amelia B. Edwards, *A Thousand Miles Up the Nile*)

*So this is dead.*

*Don't like it.*

*Wet. Heavy. Dark. Scary.*

*Alone.*

There was no floor, no walls, no ceiling, only choking, blinding rocky mud. Impossible to know which way was up or where the air was. Every time Amy's face cleared the muck, another surge slapped into her and down she went. Finally the buffeting stopped and she found herself wedged against something.

Silence. Absolute dark heavy silence.

*Am I dead? Don't want to be dead!*

*Can't be dead. Head hurts. Ribs sore. Leg twisted.*

*Not dead. Not yet.*

*'Owen? Owen, are you OK?'*

The words were a whisper at first, because she was scared to ask a question that no one would answer.

There was no Owen. This wasn't the old memory of being trapped in a crumpled car with Claire's boyfriend cold beside her and the rain sluicing down. This was a new nightmare. Where was she? What had happened?

A noise. The first noise. A phone ringing. Oh God, not another phone ringing! That did take her back to October, back to the crash, waiting waiting waiting, hoping every second to see flashing lights and the magic word Ambulance. That time her phone had been recovered from the wreckage, clogged with messages.

*Hi Amy, it's Claire, you on your way back yet? Tell Owen to stop off for some milk, OK?*

*Hey – you two taking the long way home?*

*Amy, Claire again. Pick up will ya? C'mon – I'm getting worried.*

*Amy, you call me right now, this isn't funny.*

The phone stopped ringing. Good. Noise too loud. No, there it was again. A beep. The phone, telling her she had a message. Where the hell was it? Pocket? Couldn't be there. All pockets underwater. Backpack. Yes.

Her sweater was so sodden she could hardly move. Eventually she twisted the backpack round and felt inside. *Beep*. The phone again. Found it. Flipped the lid. Light! She closed her eyes against the sudden dazzle. Cautiously opened them. Wished she hadn't. Realized where she was. Not England. Not October in the rain. Egypt. Underground. In a tomb. Resting against a coffin.

She wasn't the hysterical sort. Didn't scream or flail around, cry or faint. She stopped breathing just long enough for the knowledge to sink in then sighed. Cheating death once obviously hadn't been enough.

She swept the phone in a wide arc, using the screen light as a torch, although it was so weak it could barely push the darkness away. The tomb paintings were now dim, ghosts of godly presences, scenes of another world. Demons. Duat.

*Don't think about that.*

'Who's there?'

Someone coughed. Groaned.

Ellie! How could she have forgotten! With one hand on the coffin to steady herself, and one hand holding the phone, Amy sloshed through the waist-high water to where a dark shape was crumpled against the far wall.

*Don't be dead, don't be dead, please don't be dead.*

Ellie's eyes were closed – small mercies. Amy couldn't stand the thought of seeing another corpse's sightless stare.

'Ellie, are you dead?'

The young woman actually managed a deep, choking laugh. 'What – sort of – question – is that?' she croaked. 'And if I am, I haven't made it to paradise. Head bad. Think I hit it.' She slumped again.

'Ellie, wake up, look at me. Can you see me?'

'See you? Blinding me!'

'Sorry.' Amy closed her phone. Darkness had obviously been waiting for this moment, to fill every corner again. 'There's been an avalanche or earthquake or something. We're in the tomb, the Cat Tomb.'

Ellie swore and slid up the wall, with Amy's help, a little further out of the water. They were both clammy in the dark. She spoke with difficulty, but seemed determined to make the effort, if nothing else to reassure Amy. 'Not an avalanche. A flood. Flash flood. Rain from desert – pours into wadis, rocks, sand, everything. Bad luck to be here. Happens a coupla times a decade. Howard Carter saw one. Now us. Must've channelled through Chariot Tomb, flattened fences, found here 'n' come pouring in. You OK? You sound OK.'

'I'm fine. You . . . I think you've got concussed, or

whatever they call it. Can you walk? Can you get to the coffin?'

Again Ellie coughed up a laugh. 'Gonna bury me now, save time later?'

'No room for two,' she joked, figuring this had to be the sort of macabre humour supposed to get people through a crisis. 'You'll have to get on top and rest a bit. If you pass out in the water you'll . . . Anyway, here, I'll hoist you up. No, wait, put my sweater over it – sort of cover the decorations. I'm afraid the flowers have already crumbled. Sorry.'

'Not your fault.'

With a lot of swearing and effort Ellie got on to the coffin. She reached out in the dark to help Amy up.

'No, I can make it to where the door was, see if I can dig our way through.'

Ellie swore again. 'The water's high! Hope Farouk and Mazen are OK.'

'Typical that Dad and Jason were actually up in a *helicopter*.'

'Oh, they'll be happy they got to film the whole disaster. Wait, have you got something to dig with?'

'Hands?'

'Good luck! I'll come help in a mo. Just need to get my head steady. Hang on, I might have . . .'

Amy heard Ellie breathing hard as she searched for something. 'Hell's bells. No trowel – what sort of archaeologist am I? Got a camera, a brush and a ball of string. And hallelujah! A torch . . . that no longer works . . . Never mind. We're tough 'n' intrepid, right? Not damsels in distress, right? We'll rescue ourselves. Bloody hell, my head . . .'

Her voice trailed off.

'Ellie? Ellie?'

No reply.

Now the panic did start. Amy thrashed her way through the flood to the dense wall of debris blocking the way out of the burial chamber. She did her best to heave stones and silt aside with her bare hands. The trouble was, most of the rock fragments were quite small. When one lot was cleared, more slopped into place. It was tiring and dispiriting work, made worse by the fact that no sound came from the coffin top now.

'Ow!' Something sharp cut her palm. Stupidly, that was the one moment when she did feel like crying, like a little girl getting all weepy at the sight of blood – no one there to clean it up and kiss it better. She used her phone as a light again. Jags of turquoise pottery were responsible for the bleeding. They were pieces of a turquoise statue – what had Dad called these figurines? *Shabtis*, the magical servants of the dead. From the whip and the kilt – now cracked – she recognized it as the overseer servant, the one Dad had put over the tomb door as a joke. Now it was broken beyond repair, smashed from the surges of water and washed up amongst all the other debris.

Amy worked on. Now hot, fat tears rolled down her cheeks.

It was no good! It wasn't working! She wasn't making the slightest dent on the debris. Worse still, more water was seeping through the silt. Already she could feel it creeping up her chest, making movement more difficult. Every effort needed more gulps of stuffy air . . . and how much oxygen was left to them? Of course there'd be rescuers, somewhere in the outside world; of course they'd dig down to the tomb to find them. By the time they did, it would be too late. She and Ellie would be suffocated. Cold bodies joining the mummified Egyptian already laid out in death.

'My fault,' she snapped, speaking out loud in her anger. 'Somehow this is all my fault, like everything is. And now we're trapped and no one's coming to get us!'

The very second she said this, an arm came thrusting through the mud in front of her. She yelled as wet fingers splayed over her face.

# 25 Haunted

*Poor ghost, wandering through space! Where now are*
*thy funeral baked meats, thy changes of raiment,*
*thy perfumes and precious monuments?*
(Amelia B. Edwards, *A Thousand Miles Up the Nile*)

He fell from ashes to water. Not the cool water of a running river, not even pond water, plump with weeds. This water was a greedy whirlpool of darkness that drank him down. Sludge, silt, rocks, boxes, Shabti fought against all of them to the surface.

'Anhai?'

'Shabti?'

'Anhai!'

'Shabti! Where are you?'

'Here I am!'

Their hands met through the flood. Anhai's skin was

so fragile he thought it would tear if he held her too tightly. Although there were no lamps in the underground room, for some reason Anhai was visible, as if lit by greyness. This dull half-light spread around the chamber, like twilight through a coat of clouds.

Shabti shook his head, scattering water from his wet hair. No time to wonder about these things. They had to leave *now*. He caught Anhai up in his arms and tried to lift her clear of the water. She almost floated in his arms. Some trick of the light made her hair and fingers seem like feathers.

'Careful,' she whispered. 'Don't break me any more.'

Break her? Why would he want to do that?

He said, 'I don't know where all this water's come from – maybe the river's flooded – but there's a gate and we can get out, look, it's open!'

The metal gate was indeed unlocked and almost torn off its hinges by the forces of rocks and mud pouring through. It took a tremendous effort just to take one step towards it.

'Come on, come on, we can make it . . .'

'I can see my house,' Anhai said. She lifted her face as if drinking in imaginary light.

Shabti looked up, half expecting to see the roof of the room ripped open and the red ash of Kemet pouring through. Just rocks.

'No, there on the wall.' She pointed. 'There's my house and my gardens . . .'

'They're pictures. I've seen them already.'

'You've been here before?'

'Once . . . Hey! What was that?'

Something moved.

He spun round, making the water sluice in circles with him. Had some of Deshret's monsters followed them through the hole? Were they even now massing in the damp shadows, ready to slash their prey to pieces?

*Hush. Listen.*

Stillness. Silence.

There, again, a flash of movement, from the wall with the painting of the river scene. Most of it still showed above the flood. He stared at it like an idiot. What was wrong with the picture? The fish still swam in ripples of blue, the sky was still full of birds. There were the butterflies and dragonflies . . . the frogs and ducks. What was missing?

The cat!

The tawny cat with glittering eyes was nowhere to be seen. The cowering snake had also vanished. How was that possible? It had to be a trick of the light.

Another trick made him turn again, back to the scene

257

of the house and fields. Was that a cat prowling along the garden wall, tail straight and eyes bright? It jumped – he could have sworn he saw the cat *jump*. Where did it go? He turned once more and came face to face with the third painted wall. Was something shining there? The scene all looked the same as before – the man, the woman, the children, the . . .

. . . the sly cat under the man's chair, eyes shining as it ate from a plate of fish that seemed to bob up and down on the swell of the flood water.

Surely that was new?

Anhai shivered in his arms and shrank small. 'Do you see them? There they are! Father, mother, brother, sister. Their feet are getting wet now. Like mine. Hello, King.' The cat looked up from his silver-scaled meal. His eyes flashed gold.

'Forget your cat – we need to go!'

'He's not my cat! King doesn't belong to anyone. He only came after. Lady Cat is mine. She slept on my bed even though the doctors chased her out. I told them, "She's keeping me warm!" But they wouldn't listen. They said I should cool down. They hung wet sheets on the windows to make the air nice. Made Mother wash my skin in cold water. Made me lie under giant palm leaf fans, *swish swish swish* all through the long nights. Then

I got too cold – as cold as the mountains after sunset. I was so weak they had to force my mouth open and pour the potions in.'

Shabti shuddered to hear Anhai talk about illness. Why did the taste of a new memory make his face twist in disgust?

'Poppy juice!' he said, surprised to be thinking of it. 'I had medicine once. For bad blood . . . and pain.'

'I felt no pain. No anything after a while. Just drifting a long way away. Mother held my hand, stopped me floating off altogether. Didn't want to let me go. Was crying. They were all crying, Father, Mother, brother, sister . . . I looked down at the top of their heads. Why were they sad? Suddenly I wasn't hot or cold any more. I was better! Felt wonderful! So cool and comfortable, so light . . . I slipped out of Mother's hand and flew away as light as dust on a sunbeam . . .'

Shabti's heart chilled. What did she mean? Surely she didn't mean . . . ? Suddenly he began to understand the awful significance of the box in the next room. The body-sized box.

He was alone . . . with a ghost.

In his fright he almost dropped her, though by this time she was so light she might well have floated.

'Anhai . . . ?'

'I'm here. I've been expected in this place for so long, only somehow I lost my way.'

'Do you . . . do you remember what happened?'

She twisted in his arms and her slender hands made waves in the air. Her voice was like a sigh – a mere early morning breeze.

'*Now* I remember, when I couldn't before. All these things have been so far away. I remember the day I was leaving my family. They carried my things and so many gifts, there were priests and dancers and musicians playing. Over the river they came and the sun was so bright! I'd been through the twelve gates of darkness by then. You have to do that. Can't escape it. Then there was the dreadful palace where they tear your heart out. That's where I saw the eyes of gold and the beast with the teeth . . .'

'What beast? Where?'

'You'll see. Oh, you'll see. But I forgot about them when it was all done. I was flying so high, so free, swooping over the desert to find my family again – find myself again. They'd been keeping me safe, all wrapped in flowers and waiting. Yes, I was ready to be called down when the priests said their spells but they didn't. Couldn't. The magic snapped. Off I went, falling upwards into the sky, almost as far as the stars. I looked and looked until I forgot what I was looking for. Settled in a new house with new servants. Everything fine, everything good. But then we started slipping side to side . . . We lost the balance . . .'

The girl was going greyer every moment he stood there listening to her thoughts wafting from one memory to another. Shabti wondered, was this some dream from his poppy juice? There had been sleepless hours of muted agony, hadn't there? He remembered them now. He'd sweated in his own bed with doctors, fly swatters and wailing women . . . Some kind of accident, yes, he knew that now. Felt the horrific pain as bones snapped and his chariot shattered around him. Had he somehow wandered away from home in delirium? No. Whatever had happened since he woke up in the barley field, it hadn't been *real*, not properly real. It all had the feel of something that would ripple and vanish if he tried to look at it too closely or grasp it too tightly. He must be hallucinating, that was it.

*Wake up!*

Another flicker of movement.

The cat was back in the river scene, stalking something in the spreading fronds of a papyrus plant. No, there it was, walking towards the edge of the picture, towards the second, secret room, where Anhai's body was buried, an empty husk without its soul. Where the beast with a crocodile's mouth watched from the wall painting, waiting to devour him.

Anhai touched his face with her fingertips. 'It was you. You broke the balance. High as a hawk I looked down that dusty road and saw you racing like a storm from the desert.'

Him in a chariot. People up ahead – colours, banners, priests, music, wailing, mourners . . . a funeral procession on the west bank. On the road. In his way . . .

'I didn't mean . . . !'

'But you didn't stop.'

He got angry, really angry, aching badly and ready to fling down the hoe and be done with it all. This couldn't be true, couldn't be happening. He was still ill after the accident, that was it. The poppy juice was warping his mind, making him worry about things that couldn't possibly be true. 'Just stop talking rubbish, Anhai! We don't have time for it. We have to get out of here! We can still make it to the gate. There'll be help on the other side. Oh, I wish I could just *wake up*.'

'You're not asleep, boy. You'll never sleep again. Here, I saved something for you, boy. Look . . . Careful!'

He almost dropped the little wooden carving she pressed into his palm.

'What is it?'

'Don't you remember, it's the hedgehog from the senet board. Keep it. For luck. You'll need that.'

He disguised fear with a gruff voice. 'What do you mean?'

'There are twelve of them. Twelve demons at twelve gates. Say the spells and they'll open. I did it once. You can too. After that . . . after that it's up to you.' She tapped Shabti's chest, right over his heart.

'Fur brain!' he snorted. 'Did you drink all the beer that Hob said was missing?'

'You can still be free. Face the demons, face your judgement, then fly home to your own body – be whole again.'

One time, one last time, Shabti looked towards the open gate. It was so very tempting to shake away this bad dream, to fight through the cloying grey air to fresh air and freedom. Whatever he did, he would have to decide quickly, before the water got even higher.

'Or you can leave . . .' she whispered, her voice floating now, like a feather on the wind. 'Leave me lost again . . .'

Strangely, this only made him hold her all the more tightly. With his face buried in her fine hair, he waded through the rising water to where he knew the doorway had been. There was no hope of taking Anhai in there then saving himself. Water was pooling around his armpits as he heaved his hoe into the mud and rocks. He could only hope he would help her become whole again before it was too late and her lonely spirit faded for ever.

Heave! Heave! He worked like a slave! Then, a sudden squelching sound told him he'd somehow broken through. He pressed his hand into the muck to feel for air on the other side.

# 26 Demon Judgement

*I have come before you, my heart beating with truth,
without wrongdoing in my body, without saying falsehood
knowingly . . . May I enter into and go forth into the God's
domain, without my Ba being hindered. May I see the sun
and may I behold the moon every day.*

(Book of the Dead)

Amy staggered away from the hand groping through the
sludge. A strange grey light began to pour through the
gap in the doorway, along with new waves of water that
left her choking and struggling to keep upright.

'Jason? Mazen? Who's there?'

More debris came splashing into the thick flood. After
the flailing hand came a shoulder, a head, a chest, another
arm – all glowing in the new light. Someone appeared,
shoving muck aside with a crude wooden tool. Not Jason.

Not Mazen. Not anything like. He was a skinny minnow of a boy, with dark hair and skin streaked with mud. He seemed to be naked apart from a ragged cloth around his waist. His eyes were wide with surprise.

Amy's relief at being rescued flowered, then died. Something was wrong. Even when the water settled, the room still seemed to be sliding sideways. There was no welcome shine of electric torches or daylight, only the strange grey glow. The air, already stale, now felt full of feathers, sticking to her wet clothes and damp skin.

She meant to call for help, say they needed an ambulance for Ellie, but her voice trailed away like smoke rolling down from a spent candle. Something else was coming through the gap the boy had made. Something grey – not shadow, not light. Its eyes were small and dark, its neck stretched long and thin. A beak opened, no sound came out. Wings unfolded. Two vast grey feather cloaks spread from the bird's shoulders. Tips touched the walls of the chamber.

The heron hovered above the coffin, making the water and silt ripple with each slow beat, beat, beat of the wings. Was it real? Amy couldn't tell. One blink and it was a bird; another blink and she thought she saw a girl's pale face, framed by plaits of black hair. Stranger still, the wedjat eye shape she'd felt on top of the painted coffin now seemed to be hanging round the bird's neck, glittering with myriad colours.

The symbol of being whole.

Ellie jolted to consciousness as the bird landed. In a daze she scrambled from the coffin top and floundered in the water. She clutched Amy's arm and garbled something Amy couldn't hear above the *thump-thump-thump* of her own heartbeats.

The bird was wholly mesmerized by the serene painted smile of the face on the coffin, even when the strange boy spoke to it and caressed its feathers. Slowly, slowly the bird's wings faltered. No, Amy thought she must have imagined the bird, for there, on the coffin was a girl, shining in a simple cream-white tunic, still with the eye on a chain round her neck. No, it was definitely a bird, settling for good. Once the wings wafted, just once more. The wedjat eye flashed white, like a soundless explosion.

When next Amy looked the boy stood alone, shoulders barely out of the deep water, trembling with relief. A sweet smell of some unknown perfume filled the air. One grey feather settled on the surface of the flood.

The bird was gone.

For a few lovely moments there was peace in the underground room. The waters stilled and a soft sensation of wellbeing and *rightness* made Amy smile.

No chance to hold on to that. Darkness pressed down on them again; the ground, the walls, the very air began to shake. Ellie fell backwards against the coffin, Amy tipped forwards. The boy seized her before she submerged.

What now? A new torrent?

She fumbled for her phone. Flipped it open. Almost cried to see the light still worked.

'We have to get out, before any more water comes through!'

The boy was shaking his head. She followed his gaze forward, to the wall at the foot of the coffin. Or rather, to where the wall had been. Now she was seeing a ghostly grey river flowing through an endless emptiness. The dreary scene pulled the light from her phone, stretching it as fine as a strand of gossamer thread.

*Must turn*, she thought. *Must move. Can't move. Water rising, oh god, up to my shoulders. Move! Move!*

Everything happened very quickly after that. The darkness ahead changed. Solidified. Became two massive columns of carved green stone that reared up from nothing to become higher than the sky yet all within the stifling chamber. Hinged on the columns was a mammoth gate. The metal handles of the gate were bound with an intricate knot tied from rope thicker than Amy's arms.

'Don't do that!' she called, as if in a dream, as the boy stretched up to tug the rope.

Too late. The moment his fingers made contact a grim figure broke free from the stone of one column and took two heavy steps forward. Its face was stern and its eyes seemed to send out threads of fear to strangle them where they stood, still floundering in flood water.

Its words were mangled by carnivore teeth.

The boy flinched. His face was deathly white. He could not speak.

*What does it mean?* Amy panicked. *Some kind of challenge? Or a question. It's a gatekeeper! What do I know about gates? Something I read recently . . .*

It was a struggle to put thoughts together, like threading tiny beads on a fragile thread. Then her mind suddenly glittered with ideas.

*Joking with Jason. What about?* Duat, *that was it – the twelve gates of Duat. Duat for Dummies, ha ha, wait –* spells! *Spells were buried with the mummy so it could, what? Get past the guardians to . . . Can't remember. Never mind about that. We needed to say a spell, the right spell . . . Where can I find spells? In the coffin? Not looking in there! The* Book of the Dead! *In my bag. Ellie! Ellie! Get my backpack – it's on the coffin!*

She couldn't turn her thoughts to words and had to feel

through the flood herself until she found the fabric of her bag. The book was soaked, of course, and the pages were stuck together.

*Come on, come on, Amy, you can do this. Find the page, the first gate, what do I say? What do I say?*

She glanced up and saw that the statue had raised a spear tipped with black obsidian. The point grazed the bare skin of the boy's chest. His back was straight but terror gripped him tight.

*Terror!* The name of the first gatekeeper, she remembered now. But what about the rest of the spell?

In her haste she ripped a couple of pages. Found the right ones. Shone her feeble phone light on to them. Read aloud. Had a sudden bizarre anxiety that she wouldn't be understood. Her voice was quickly lost in the flow of the ghostly river.

'Hail to you gods! I know you and know your names. I shall not fall down in fear of you. You shall not accuse me of crime! I know you! I know you and know your names. I shall not fall down in fear of you!'

*Maybe not fall, but certainly shake. Oh god oh god, it's looking at me again. What do I say now? What do I say? The light's fading – I can't read any more.*

A new voice wavered. Some way behind, Ellie had woken to this strange dream. As if in a trance she recited the spell to challenge the guardian of the first gate.

'Oh Power of Destruction, whose words repel storms, the name of the gatekeeper is Terror.'

Ellie's voice was weak, but Terror heard its name spoken. Names were powerful things. They could open gates, make people immortal . . . or call them to judgement. The spear straightened. The massive knot on the gate began to uncoil like a restless snake. The rope fell away and the great gate swung open, screaming on its hinges. Strangely, none of the flood water in the burial chamber flowed through.

A new gate appeared fully formed in an instant. It was lit by the glow of two orange and blue columns, crested by a row of rearing cobras. The second gatekeeper was a fearsome female as bright and endless as a world without horizons, with eyes as sharp as black glass.

Ellie raised herself to standing and spoke the spell. Her words cracked. Amy had to repeat the gatekeeper's name – *Lady of the Sky*. As before, the demon deferred to them, the massy gate opened and they were pulled through.

At the third gate the keeper was also bold and brilliant to behold and his name was *Splendid*. Amy shouted the spell out as soon as Ellie murmured it. She jolted to hear the boy at her side pick up on the last word and shout it too. By the fourth gate he was standing taller. Hearing the spell from Ellie, he garbled the words with Amy: 'Oh mighty of Knives, the one who smashes the enemies, the name of the gatekeeper is Long-Horned Bull.'

Slowly, gravely the bull-headed guardian stood back for the gate to open.

Spells turned away knives at the fifth gate and made numberless snakes at the sixth crawl away. Seven, eight, nine, ten . . . Ellie pulled spells from her memory and the two children flung them at whatever grotesque guardian stood in their way. Gate after gate loomed, unlocked and opened. Eleven, twelve . . . the last gate was faced, the last guard overcome. By then it was too late to be thinking, *I don't want to be here at all*. Wherever they had arrived, there was no going back.

This final gate was the largest and grandest of them all, but it still swung open as lightly as if made of paper. Beyond this gateway the light shone green. Not a sickly green, or the colour of poison. This was the green of unripened wheat, fresh-cut grass or fat autumn apples.

Amy blinked. After so many hideous demon guardians, this wasn't the kind of hell she'd been expecting. Was she supposed to go in? She looked at the boy. There was sad resignation in his eyes. She reached for his hand. Ellie seemed to fall away, like a forgotten fragment of a dream.

They had arrived in a palatial chamber with a fire-red roof and a floor that shimmered like turquoise water. Godly figures sat on innumerable green thrones, all facing a great carved canopy so grand and golden Amy couldn't see beyond the dazzle to who was revered inside.

That hardly mattered. She was far more concerned about the scene directly in front of her.

First, there were weighing scales. Not the neat digital sort she was used to back home. These were huge balancing scales – two metal pans hanging from a horizontal beam. Where had she seen something similar? On a statue? Yes, a statue with one arm upraised and scales held out. It was the symbol of justice. This was it. End of journey. Dazzling judge, the seated jury . . . and there could be no doubt which ghastly creature played the part of executioner. It actually crouched beneath the scales as if ready to pounce and devour. It had a green reptilian face like a crocodile, with red scales on its throat and a mane like a lion's, only striped blood-red and green. The tawny lion's body had thin, clawed forepaws but sturdy hind legs that could stamp on giants as if they were ants. Head turning sideways, one red eye looked straight at the children.

'Ammut!' the boy whispered in horror.

Another figure stepped forward, tall and stately with

neatly pleated clothes. Every time Amy blinked she saw the head change, from human to jackal-faced, like Mazen's dog. *Anubis* – that was the name that came to mind. Beyond Anubis, another figure with a beak held a pen and ink palette. It had a large *ankh* amulet hanging from its chest. Thoth, the scribe.

Thoth looked at Amy then down a list on a papyrus scroll, as if searching for her name.

Her eyes bristled with tears. She realized, it's *me* they're going to judge. They'll weigh me in the balance and find me wanting.

Every little lie, every bit of bad behaviour, she felt them all float to the surface of her mind to be skimmed off and judged. Recent memories surged up as a thick flood: Owen alive and well. *Live life to the full*, he always said. So big and warm – hugging Claire, playing football in the back garden. But what had she done? Something so stupid, so small in itself. Got stuck in town that night, after a movie with the gang. Spent her bus money on chips. On a bloody bag of chips and a can of drink. Sure, said Owen, I'll come pick you up, no prob, Claire's only making me look at bridal magazines anyway, sit tight, I'll be right over.

And he was, driving her back home through the country lanes, favourite music playing, lights on full beam, laughing, joking, doing all the things you can do when you're still alive.

It was a head-on collision. An old car – no airbags. Amy cracked her ribs against the taut seat belt. Bashed her head on the dashboard. Twisted her legs as the car spun round. By then Owen was already losing brain through his broken skull. He was out in the rain, right out through the windscreen. No seat belt. Living life on the edge . . . then not living at all.

She felt a black slick of guilt spreading out around her. *My fault. All my fault.*

High on their seats the solemn godly figures leaned forwards.

Thoth tipped his head like an inquisitive bird then shook it very slightly. There was no mistaking the gesture. *Not you.*

'But . . .'

Again the shaking head. Again the *no.*

'. . . it was all my fault . . .'

*No. Not you.*

The creature's expression clearly said – *dismissed. Not guilty.*

Amy could have laughed with surprise and relief, or at the very least cried for a century, but then she saw that the stern figure was still pointing. Not at her any more.

The accusation was against the boy instead.

The boy didn't, or couldn't, move. He stood before the judge, jury and executioner, ready to accept whatever happened, as if he somehow knew he deserved his fate.

Jackal-headed Anubis loomed by the scales. A feather floated down gently and landed in one tray, barely making it quiver.

'That's hardly fair!' Amy blurted out. 'Almost everything's heavier than a feather!'

What could they possibly put in the other tray that wouldn't weigh it down?

Anubis spread out a slender hand. Searching fingers reached right to the boy's bare chest. They didn't stop there. Anubis pushed his hand through the skin and ribs, nudged aside the lungs and found what it was looking for. The fingers closed around the boy's heart and slowly drew it out of his body. When the fingers uncurled the heart showed on the palm, not bloody but glowing.

Gently Anubis placed it in the empty tray of the scales.

# 27 The Akh

*Who is this Great Tom Cat? He is the God Ra himself.*

(Coffin Texts, Spell 335)

Shabti looked down at his chest, expecting to see a gaping wound. Nothing. Felt around his mind for understanding. Again, nothing.

Time hushed and dwindled to one, silent moment. Only the heart moved, gently beating in the empty tray of the scales. He watched it with detached curiosity. It seemed transparent at first, then he saw colours and shapes moving inside. People he knew, places he recognized. One after the other, his life's memories unfurled and faded. He was drawn to them with a dreamy compulsion, like a poppy juice addict wanting more black drops of the seductive pain killer.

There he was as a toddler, laughing at his pet monkey.

Older next, having his first riding lesson. Reading stories by lamplight – skipping to the end to find out what happened. Playing senet – cheating sometimes. Running through fields with a whip and top, calling to his friends, going faster, faster, faster so he'd be first.

A bow and spear – he saw these weapons again, both the wooden toys he first wielded, then the proper full-sized versions. Hour after hour, day after day, the memories showed his training. Sweat and blood stung his skin, but never tears. Not those. No Young Hero would ever show such weakness. Head high he accepted all the honours and praise due to one of his rank and achievement.

Stepped up into his chariot.

It was a beauty, that speed machine. Advanced wickerwork body with supple hafts and perfect wheels. Light, balanced, lethal. With the best horses, of course, majestic high-steppers that could gallop like the wind.

Oh. Galloping horses.

Bad memory. Hooves pounded through his head, dragging him along a road towards events he'd long been trying to hide from. He couldn't rein them in, couldn't stop that headlong race towards his conscience.

There in the gods' chamber he flung an arm over his eyes. Even then he saw clearly. He was back inside the memory, back in his chariot on a rocky road. First he noticed the clouds of dust kicked up by a procession along the road ahead. He certainly wasn't going to stop. Let them get out of his way! Didn't they know who he was? *Move for me!*

He'd spurred the horses on, not knowing that each crack of the whip would be repaid by lashes on his own skin from Master Hob in Kemet.

In Duat every excruciating detail of the crash was felt again. The description was written, painfully, on his own heart. He saw people fling down their palm banners and garlands. Dancers leaped for safety, musicians played a final discordant note. A priest tried to block him from the painted coffin.

Too late Shabti pulled his horses back. They reared, tangling their traces. First one crumpled, then the other. He felt more of a pang for them than himself as the chariot was wrenched on to its side and he was dragged along with the splintering wreckage. That was when bones cracked and his skull dented. A red haze covered his eyes. He lay in the ruins of his arrogance, watching one chariot wheel slowly turning, spoke after spoke after spoke after spoke after . . .

The memories were fresher after that. He was waking up in a barley field, following the white hippopotamus, working for Hob, hiding in the garden . . . all the awful marvellous things that had happened to bring him to this moment of judgement. Had they been real?

As real as the little wooden hedgehog in his hot hand.

His thoughts became bitter. He should have slowed, should have stopped sooner. In his pride he'd thought he was invulnerable, immortal. Not so. Crashing into the funeral procession broke the bonds between Anhai's body and her *ba*. At least he'd been able to help her become whole again. Whether she'd forgiven him or not, she was gone. He was alone at the moment of his judgement.

Not that it mattered. He was only one breath from watching his heart weigh down the scales. He deserved to be devoured. Nameless. Forgotten.

He bowed his head in utter, humbling regret.

The moment of time passed.

The scales trembled.

Ammut the Devourer licked her crocodile lips as the dish with Shabti's heart began to sink down. Shabti closed his eyes. *Let it be over quickly*, that's all he could hope for. After that, he wouldn't have to suffer, wouldn't have anything. Total extinction. Never again remembered in all the ages of the earth.

No teeth crunched.

His heart was not so heavy. The scales drew level again. Balance was restored. The feather itself glowed so brightly it was lost in the general brilliance of the gods' court.

The god Anubis bowed to him. The god Thoth scratched a line across a name on his papyrus scroll. The god Osiris, Lord of the Dead, lifted his hand in dismissal.

It was done.

Ammut waddled backwards into shadow.

'Go,' said Thoth. His bird eyes were black and bright. 'Take back your heart and be whole.'

Even as Shabti looked down in wonder, his spirit was removed from the scales and gently pushed back into his chest, where it began to throb with painful happiness. He blinked, like a silly boy who hasn't been listening properly to his teacher.

'Excuse me, but, where shall I go?'

No reply.

He found he was standing on nothing, surrounded by nothing. Looking at nothing. Thoth, Anubis, all the gods, gateways and guardians were gone. The foreign girl had gone too, tumbling into some invisible flood. He wished he could have thanked her for helping him through the gates. Wondered what would happen to her.

'Just me,' he said out loud. 'Is this eternity, this night without stars?'

Something soft and furry tickled his cheek.

Catching his breath, hope made him reach out and feel the space where air should have been. A long grey thread hung down before him, just like the fur from Ta Miu that had helped him through the hole in Anhai's garden.

*Shall I?*

He took hold of the thread and tugged once. It didn't collapse around him – had to be fastened to something, but what?

*Why not climb up and see?*

It shouldn't have been possible, the long monkey-wriggle up the thread to the top of the sky. With every effort the nothing around him seemed less desolate, until he thought he could see colour. At first it was the deep blue of midnight, pricked by cold stars. Then came the rose of dawn and the warm orange of early sun. The sun grew gold and strong, and he climbed straight towards it. His strength never seemed to fail, no matter how high he climbed. He stopped once, when something small fell the impossibly long distance down into nothingness. He'd lost the tiny wooden hedgehog. Should he go back and find it?

The sun's light drew him further on and further up.

He knew his eyes should have been burned beyond their sockets. Instead, he found they were greedy for the sunlight. In it he saw new lines and shapes. Soon he was thinking it wasn't the sun but a ship, a splendid royal barque, made of turquoise, jasper, emeralds and lapis lazuli. It was complete with gleaming sails, coiled golden ropes and stacked harpoons, ready for the hunt. Sailors moved about the boat, setting the course across the sky. One small figure was seated at the prow, another familiar shape waited at the helm.

Strong arms helped him over the edge of the boat. Close to, he could see how beautifully the golden wood was polished and how perfect all the joints were. The furry grey thread shimmered and disappeared once he was safely aboard.

'Welcome,' said a warm voice. 'Welcome and well done. Out of great wrong you have made a right. My ship sails smoothly and the way is clear.'

Shabti looked around. Who spoke? He saw only a cat at the helm. He was very glad King was looking so alive and well. Had any cat ever been bigger or glossier?

'The snake didn't eat you!' he exclaimed.

King yawned. 'Apophis can be chastened.'

'Can't you kill it? Stop it ruining things, like Kemet and the white house?'

'What has been ruined? Places that have no earthly reality. Houses and fields of the mind. Like time, they don't exist. You don't need them now, you are here with me. As for Chaos, we hunt it, but Chaos shouldn't be killed, otherwise order would cease to exist. Day and night, strong and weak, life and death. Each one needs the other. For twelve hours I fight my battles, going down into the underworld to face the twelve guardians of the gates. This time you helped me, and you won through. Now we have the twelve hours of daylight when I shine over the land and entice life out of the dust.'

'I was . . . wrong, though. Bad. You must have seen my memories. What I did. It was my fault, about Anhai's *ba* being broken away from her body. She was nearly gone for ever. Is she . . . is she really whole again?'

King's tail twitched once. 'You have been arrogant and humble, cowardly and brave. Brave when you didn't know you ought to be and when your fear was at its strongest. Yes, you were most of all brave. Your heart was weighed with the Maat feather, which represents truth and justice. The scales were even. There was balance.'

The great cat jumped from its seat and actually

twined itself round Shabti's legs, purring. That was when Shabti realized he wasn't caked in mud, blood and sweat. His rags had been replaced by a shining white kilt. Around his neck was a thick collar, fashioned in the shape of opening lotus flowers. Hanging from the collar was a golden wedjat eye – sign of healing and being whole.

'Am I whole?' he asked in wonder. He already knew the answer. He felt marvellous! 'I don't understand.'

'You are small and imperfect,' said King. He leaped to the highest spar of the sails. 'I am RA! The Great Tom Cat!'

'There was a girl,' Shabti called up anxiously. 'She helped me get through the twelve gates, it wasn't just me. Will she be all right, too?'

'Nothing to do with you now.'

'But the missing things, the underground room . . .'

'As I said, not your concern. Let others find their own balance. You have helped the person you were meant to help and in doing so have saved yourself.'

King sprang from the spar over the side of the boat. Anxiously Shabti looked for him . . . only to marvel as the cat appeared again, with a star-bright fish wriggling in his jaws.

'He does that,' said another voice, one that warmed

his heart more than any sun. 'Always jumping around like a mad thing, then curling up for a snooze when he thinks no one's looking.'

'Anhai! You're here too! That's wonderful. I was afraid you didn't . . . Where are we? I don't understand.'

She looked amazing – so bright and bold. So very *present*. She patted a space at the prow for him. 'Don't try to understand. Just be.'

'Yes,' said the cat, now sounding monumental. 'You have passed through seasons of millions and hundreds of thousands of moments. Now you shall simply be, for millions and millions of years, a lifetime of millions of years. Your bodies and *ba* are bonded. Leave your husks behind, and your false images of life as it was. You have become an *Akh*, a spirit judged and found to be true. You travel with me now. I am Lord of the Sunbeams! I have come to lighten the darkness and it is bright! Those who were in darkness have given praise to me. The doors of the sky are opened for me. By night this boat shines as a star, by day as the sun. It is a matter a million times true!'

There should have been at least a million questions boiling in Shabti's head, but he found that as the boat surged forwards on a turquoise stream, all the tumbling experiences he'd had resolved into one simple query.

'Please, sir,' he said. 'Please – may I know my name now?'

The cat's eyes twinkled. He came bounding over to the two children, jumped on the boy's shoulder – it was no longer sore – and he whispered one word.

*Strong.*

With that the boy felt as clear as sunlight, through and through.

# 28 Daylight

*The doors of the sky are opened for me.*

(*Book of the Dead*)

Like scarab babies scrabbling into their first sunlight, fingers pushed up through the rocky ground. An arm, a head, another arm followed.

'Hello! Hello! Help!'

At first the voice was as faint as the sound of sand sliding down a slope, and there was no wind in the wadi to carry it. If Farouk and Mazen weren't already searching close by they would never have heard it. Anubis barked loudly. His paws kept sinking in the soft ground. Farouk and Mazen skidded to their knees and used pieces of scrap wood to clear away stones and sludge around the collapsed tomb entrance. Gradually they hoisted the mud-sodden figure out. Ellie collapsed on to her belly and coughed up dirty water. All the while she gestured back to the hole she'd escaped from.

Farouk's voice was rougher than usual. 'The other one, is she . . . ?'

Mazen didn't even wait to ask. He was back on hands and knees in the mud, with Anubis digging at his side. More mud slopped into the hole. Beyond that was silent water and darkness.

Ellie pushed matted curls from her eyes and joined her rescuers.

'Pulled Amy into antechamber,' she gasped. 'Too heavy to drag out.'

Mazen called into the shadows: 'Amy! Amy!'

'She wasn't moving. No pulse.'

Farouk snapped out instructions in Arabic. Mazen was so nervous, his words fluttered like caged starlings. Neither of them could squeeze through the gap into the tomb and it was taking too long to make the hole wider. Even as they made the desperate attempt to reach Amy's body, more flood water was seeping through layers of porous rock.

Then they heard a new sound. Ellie looked up, fearing another tumult of disaster was about to come pouring down on them, but it was actually the sound of helicopter blades churning up the air. The helicopter dropped low, lifted up, then finally landed on a narrow stretch of valley floor not wrinkled with new rivers of rock. Even before the blades stopped rotating two people jumped out and began to run. Ellie tried to wave them back. It was too treacherous! The runners floundered in banks of wet sand, sinking in knee-deep, even thigh-deep in places. The helicopter rose again but it could only hover close by. There was nowhere nearer to land.

Jason was younger and fitter, but he didn't get there much faster than Tony Clayton, whose face would have been red with exertion, if it wasn't white from dread.

'Amy?' was the only word he could manage.

Ellie shook her head. 'We were in the tomb when the flood came. I'll go in again and we can all pull her out.'

'I'll go!' said Clayton.

'We will go,' said Farouk and Mazen together.

Jason was ahead of them, already sliding into the hole legs first. He held on to the wooden lintel of the tomb doorway to stop himself falling all the way in. 'Tie something to the metal bar of the gate, then pass me the end!'

They ripped a thick strip from the bottom of Mazen's galabeya. Jason tested the knot round his waist. 'Thank God for my scout training. It'll hold.'

He was lowered into the gloom. The water was a

horrible shock to his sun-warm skin and with every step he took, he imagined snakes coiling round his submerged body. He had a torch in his free hand. It illuminated the awful destruction of the Cat Tomb, and the sad colours of the wall paintings as the water lapped over them. He yelped as something heavy floated into him, and stupidly dropped the torch. It splashed and vanished. His fingers felt a cold face and wet hair. Amy!

Someone tugged on the makeshift rope.

'Pull us up!' he shouted.

The knot held but the fabric ripped. Three times he struggled to push Amy's dead-weight body up into daylight. Twice he slipped and fell back into the murk. On the third attempt he realized she was actually moving – fighting him off, in fact.

'Amy, it's me!'

'Can . . . rescue myself . . . thank you – very – much.'

Amy didn't even realize her eyes had been closed until she opened them. She'd been seeing strange visions of stars in a night-blue sky, hearing the creak of wooden oars and the slap of sail fabric blowing taut. Then she felt full sunshine chiselling under her eyelashes. She looked and saw she was out in daylight – glorious, blinding, heartening daylight. A shadow fell across her face.

'Amy? Open your eyes. Look at me, Munchkin. It's Dad. You've had a bump on the head. Can you see how many fingers I'm holding up?'

Her eyes were stinging from all the sand in the water. She squinted and mumbled, 'Twenty.'

'Good. You're obviously all right. I just need to know a couple of things . . .' Her dad took her through a concussion checklist with the surprising professionalism of a trained first-aider. Then, and only then, did he squash her into a suffocating hug. 'Turn the bloody camera off!' he snapped at Kev. 'Can't you see this isn't telly now?'

Amy let the sun warm her through and through. For all she kept telling her dad she was fine, her thoughts wouldn't quite come down out of the sky and settle in her mind again. Part of her felt as if she were climbing high into unseen stars. Despite the hugs and general gladness, she was aware of missing something precious. Memories, bad and good, seemed to have been washed away by the dark water underground.

Ellie was suddenly at her side, ridiculously happy now that Amy was seen to be alive and well.

'I couldn't get you all the way out,' she kept saying. 'I tried, but I wasn't strong enough.'

Amy shook her head and droplets of water sparkled in

her hair like diamonds. 'Not your fault,' she said. 'I thought you were dead too, when you fainted.'

'Fainted? I don't remember that. I remember the flood crashing into the burial chamber, then next thing I was pulling you through the gap in the broken doorway and trying to get you to the entrance gate.' A curious look passed over her face – doubt mingled with excitement. 'What do *you* remember then?'

*What do I remember?* Amy closed her eyes. Like all vivid dreams, images of this one were fleeting. They all but vanished as her dad jostled closer and began pouring a bottle of water over her forehead.

'Dad! Ow!'

'Nasty cut you've got there.' He dabbed at it carefully. 'What's all this about the burial chamber? What were you doing in there?'

Ellie frowned. 'The doorway was broken,' she said.

'By the force of the flood?'

'No, but . . .'

Amy's dad shrugged that off and turned to his daughter. 'Best we get back to the hotel and sort you out. Fancy a trip in the helicopter, eh, Munchkin?' He got to his feet, grunting, and grabbed Farouk's arm. 'You're a good man, Farouk. The best overseer I ever worked with. We flew over your village on our way back here. The floods missed it, but you'd better head off to your families. God – look at this place. It's a total disaster area! Ruined – all of it. I thought I invited my daughter to visit an excavation, not to *be* one! In future, let's hope we get a little more archaeology, and a little less action, eh? But thanks, Farouk. And you too, Mazen. Thank you.'

Farouk acknowledged the gratitude, and let his hand be shaken vigorously.

For the first time Amy looked out over the distorted landscape of the wadi.

Floods from the desert plateau had coursed through cliff fissures and crevasses, finding the quickest way. The Chariot Tomb had obviously funnelled one torrent of rock-laden water down the slope and straight to the Cat Tomb enclosure. Sections of fence, buckets, tables, crates . . . all were jumbled in the mud, a uniform reddish-brown colour.

'How did you know?' she asked Mazen in wonder. 'How did you even know where to look, it's all so . . . the same under the mud?'

'Cat,' said Mazen immediately.

'You mean Anubis?'

'No. Not the dog. Cat. Here.' He reached inside his ruined galabeya and pulled out something small and white. A limestone fragment with a picture of a tawny tom cat. 'Cat foot shows dig here.'

Amy tried to catch Ellie's eye, but her dad had commandeered the young archaeologist. Once the first shock of the disaster was over, his mind was as busy as a beetle, wondering what he'd missed below ground.

'I know the camera was ruined,' he began, 'but surely you managed to salvage something from inside the actual burial chamber. What was it like in there? Did we hit jackpot?'

Ellie's description began confidently, as she told him about the wooden sarcophagus and the funerary garlands. When she got to descriptions of the wall paintings – the scenes of Am Duat – her voice faltered a little.

'And there was a bird, I think. The Egyptian benu bird. Yes, I definitely saw a painting of a grey heron over the coffin. But it was dark after that! You can't expect me to remember. I don't know! I told you, the whole place is filled with water. I was busy trying to get us both out before we ran out of air . . .'

'Oh, I couldn't be more grateful for that, only I just wondered . . .' His shoulders slumped. 'Never mind. We'll just rewrite the end of the episode. Do some blah about the forces of nature burying the dead once more, leaving them in eternal silence, etc., etc. Yes, it'll be good to get a shot of Jason knee-deep in debris at the ruined entrance – the living boy standing over the dead boy . . .'

'Actually, Tony, it was a girl buried there.'

'How d'you know?'

'The name, Tony. *Lady Anhai*, written everywhere on the walls. It was a bit of a giveaway . . .'

Listening to them both argue again, Amy relaxed a little. Everything was falling back towards normal. She stretched her neck to get more sun on her face, just like the first time she'd been alone in the wadi, when she'd felt like a small grain of sand on the crust of a vast planet spinning in space . . . when she'd found the strange cat cartoon . . .

A little confused, she realized she was holding something quite tightly in one hand. It couldn't be the limestone fragment. She'd obviously dropped that going into the Cat Tomb before the flood, which was how Mazen had come to find it again. No, this was something small and knobbly. She uncurled her fingers. Her heart gave an extra deep thump when she saw what it was – a little wooden hedgehog, just like the pieces found with the senet board game. Odd to think she must have somehow seized hold of it in the darkness and kept it safe.

Then she became conscious of something more bulky in her pocket and she heard a little electronic beep.

Impossible! She worked her mobile out of her sodden black jeans.

Jason crouched down beside her. 'I guess you nearly were buried with your phone after all,' he said.

She was embarrassed by new warmth in his voice and the look in his eyes that said, *Thank God you're still alive*.

'No kidding. I can't believe it's still working. It used to conk out at even the slightest hint of drizzle.' She looked over to where her dad was staring gloomily at the destruction of his *Action Archaeology!* dream. A few photos of the burial chamber would make a nice late Christmas present for him. She flipped the phone lid to see how the pictures had turned out. A frown crinkled her forehead. 'I could've sworn my phone rang while I was down there. And it did. Look.'

*1 New Message.*

She clicked on the envelope icon. A big smile broke across her face as she read the news from Claire.

# 29 Immortality

*I shall have power in my heart,*
*I shall have power in my arms,*
*I shall have power in my legs,*
*I shall have power to do whatever*
*I desire; my ba and my corpse*
*Shall not be restrained at the portals*
*Of the West when I go in or out in peace.*

(*Book of the Dead*, Spell 26)

England had the driest winter on record, followed by a summer of endless blue skies. Rain started to fall in autumn, just in time to turn the fiery fallen leaves into gutter-clogging mulch. The dales and moors of Yorkshire drank the water greedily. Lawns revived, reservoirs filled, and umbrella sales rocketed. Amy refused to carry one.

'Can't you park the car a bit closer to the museum?' she complained.

Her dad snapped, 'I could if every single person in the whole of Harrofield hadn't turned up for this bloody exhibition.' He contemplated risking a ticket on double yellow lines. 'You shouldn't've worn so much make-up.'

'It's waterproof.'

'I'll carry the brolly,' Claire called from the back of the car. 'You can take the baby instead.'

'What if she's sick?'

'You're never sick on mummy, are you, Darling?'

Amy twisted round in her seat to watch her sister tickle the baby until it hiccupped with joy. Claire still had her dark days, and she'd disappeared with the baby on the anniversary of the car crash, returning late at night with red eyes, but she had a wonderful ability to squeeze every possible moment of fun out of a day. *Live while you're alive*, was her motto, always accompanied by a hug so warm it killed any doubts or fears in Amy's heart.

When Amy got the text from Claire to say the baby was born, it had simply said: *It's early and it's a girl!*

Owen had died before choosing a name for the unborn child. Grandma Clayton suggested Petula, after one of her dogs. Tony Clayton voted for Hatshepsut, the famous female pharaoh. Claire thanked them graciously but said she was quite taken with the name of the long-gone Egyptian girl who'd so nearly shared her burial chamber with Amy. And so the baby was Anhai.

Rain kept pounding down on the car roof, beating the same rhythm Amy had heard the night of the crash. Now she barely felt the ache of old wounds. It was hard to dwell on Owen's death when his daughter was so very much alive and lovely.

Amy's dad tucked his shirt into his overextended cummerbund. 'Everybody out! I don't care if you wear flippers to cross the road, just get moving before Ellie comes and blames *me* for the fact we're late for her opening night.'

He glanced up at the glossy white banner stretching across Harrofield museum's classical façade:

*BEYOND THE GRAVE – The Afterlife in Ancient Egypt*

The car door opened on Amy's side. Jason Henderson looked in, not a speckle of rain showing on his smart suit.

'Are you getting out or what? Nice outfit.'

Jason's eyes moved up Amy's legs to her face. He smiled. He had an umbrella.

They splashed across the street to the museum steps, where Amy was to wait while Jason escorted the others over.

A skinny man with a massive camera jerked his head towards her. 'Mind if I take a picture?'

She looked round. No, he wasn't talking to anyone else. 'My dad's the one from *Action Archaelogy*!'

'Yeah, I'll get them too, but you're that girl, aren't you?'

*That girl?* Which girl? The one who made the headlines after the horrific car accident? The one who went to Egypt and almost got drowned?

'. . . the one who found the things in the exhibition . . .' the photographer gushed. 'I just had a sneak preview – fantastic! Stand still – smile!'

*I don't smile*, she wanted to say. *I might have lippy on my teeth*. But she let him take the pictures anyway. She knew she looked good in the black leather biker jacket, the boots, the leggings, and the candy pink froth of tulle that somehow passed for a skirt.

'Hey!' The photographer grinned even more as the rest of Amy's group sought shelter between the entrance columns. 'You're that boy, right? The one who rescued this lass here. I saw you on TV.'

'I didn't exactly rescue her,' Jason said through gritted teeth. Amy's heel had just stamped on his toes. Hard. 'She mostly rescued herself.'

'Excuse me . . . can I just take your names for the local paper . . . ?'

Jason dragged Amy inside.

Baby Anhai blew bubbles of spit at the photographer then produced her most enchanting smile.

'Takes after her bloody granddad,' laughed Claire.


The museum was bright, warm and welcoming. Amy was amazed to see how the main gallery had been transformed. One wall was dominated by a vast projection of sunset over the west bank of the Nile, at Thebes. How well she remembered those shapes and red shadows. She half expected to see the silhouette of a black jackal high on the desert edge.

'My second favourite place in the world,' Jason murmured.

'I've already guessed your first favourite place is the mummy room at the British Museum,' she gloated.

'Actually, no. I've got a new first favourite place now.' He squeezed her hand, but didn't get time to elaborate. Amy's dad yanked him away for a special *Action Archaeology!* publicity shot.

Amy escaped. She wanted to see more of the exhibition, to seek out the blue lotus jar, the clay lamp, the wooden hedgehog . . . She paused by a grainy photograph. Why had they included something of such poor quality in such a classy display about tomb art? Oh.

She realized what the picture was. She'd taken it herself, underground in the Cat Tomb, using only her mobile phone. It showed a grey-white image, named as a heron, or benu-bird. The painting outline was blurred and the lighting so poor, it looked as if the grey heron were hovering just in front of itself.

She shook off more memories. There was something else she was eager to see . . . Ellie would show her where it was now displayed.

She found Ellie drinking champagne with the other museum curators. They could tell from the buzz of the opening night that the exhibition was going to be a great success.

'Hey, Ellie – this all looks fantastic. Thanks for the invite.'

'Amy! Brilliant. Come and meet the team . . . Everyone, this is Tony Clayton's daughter Amy – she's personally responsible for leading us to half the amazing objects on display here.' Once the introductions were done, and Amy's blushes had subsided, Ellie grabbed her a champagne and led her into the maze of exhibits. 'You said you wanted to see the shabti, right?'

Amy nodded. The shabti was just one of many items on loan from Cairo. It was a turquoise figurine, barely seventeen centimetres high. She'd only spotted it during her very last minute in the Windy Wadi, as she floundered to the helicopter through the rivers of churned-up sand and rocks that had poured through the Chariot Tomb. The shabti figure held a hoe and a basket. The hieroglyph spells on its front were as clear to read as the day they were carved. The little thing looked ready to leap up and answer, *Here I am!* Most significantly, it carried its owner's name, in all probability the name of the boy from the Chariot Tomb.

*Nakht* – the ancient Egyptian word for strong.

'It *is* in the exhibition, isn't it?' Amy asked. 'Jason said Cairo Museum had been pretty generous.'

Ellie got a sudden sparkle in her eyes. 'Oh, Cairo have been more than generous. We have the shabti on show all right, but look what else they've loaned us . . . Our very own expert!'

They rounded a corner and almost collided with a very elegant lady dressed in a vintage Chanel suit.

'Dr Hassan!'

'Nice to meet you again, Amy.'

They shook hands politely, then Ellie linked her arm through the scientist's and explained. 'I got an email from Rosa saying she'd been offered a job in the middle of nowhere – some wilderness. I thought she meant she'd be X-raying mountain mummies in Peru, or Yemen, or something, then next thing I know she's asking if York University was anywhere in my precious *Yorkshire*.'

Rosa smiled. 'Since then I was kidnapped and brought to Harrofield to help with the exhibition. I have been promised endless cups of tea and snow at Christmas. But, Amy, I've been waiting for you, to show you this . . .'

She stepped to one side.

Amy saw a blank widescreen TV. Surely they weren't going to make her sit through the award-winning episode of *Action Archaeology!* in Egypt? Hadn't she already watched it enough times, with Mum, Claire, Grandma Clayton and the dogs yapping through all the commentary, not to mention baby Anhai gurgling? Plus there'd been that one time with Jason, although to be fair, they hadn't paid the TV much attention . . .

The screen lightened. She gasped as a skull appeared. A few more people came closer to see what was happening. The image of the skull rotated.

'It looks real,' she said, tempted to reach out and touch it.

Ellie explained. 'All the images scanned that day in TT439, they're made into a 3D composite.'

'This is the mummy from the Chariot Tomb?'

'Watch.'

Slowly the image evolved. Strange sticks appeared,

jutting from points all over the skull bones and the jaw.

'Marker points,' Ellie said, 'to show the depth of muscle and skin. Amazing, isn't it? Rosa wouldn't let me see it all till tonight – said it'd be a surprise.'

Layer by layer, bare muscles and tendons attached themselves. By the time the skull was covered, a crowd of people were watching the animation. When the skin went on, the face looked less grotesque. There were even holes in the earlobes, where pierced earrings had once hooked through.

Amy felt a shiver start at the base of her spine and come tingling all the way to full consciousness. The face – it looked familiar!

Rosa spoke to everyone. 'The information you see has been collected from X-rays and CAT scans of the original body, also, from photographs and film footage. That is how we know how to position the eyebrows exactly.' In death, the mummy's hair had been sparse and wispy. In recreated life, the boy on the TV screen had springy black hair. 'For the eye colour, we guessed brown, like most Egyptian people.'

It was the eyes that drew Amy most. She felt as if she'd seen that look before – that clear gaze and haughty expression.

The image stopped rotating and the boy looked out at

all of them. In a final trick of CGI the image smiled once then faded. There was a spontaneous burst of applause from everyone who watched. Everyone except Amy and Ellie. Amy glanced over at the young archaeologist and wondered if her own face looked so pale and haunted.

Rosa's voice broke the spell. 'So there we have it – the centrepiece for the exhibition. This incredible computer reconstruction has given life *beyond the grave* to a boy who died many centuries ago.'

More applause.

Amy didn't hear it. She pushed her way through the guests and found Jason. He gave her a kiss on her neck in gratitude for being rescued from a queue of *Action Archaeology!* fans, who all wanted autographs and a photo with their idol. He linked his fingers with hers.

'It's all looking fantastic, isn't it? Apart from that little domestic scene over there, where half the Clayton family are ruthlessly attacking the buffet table. I guess baby Anhai likes falafel.'

'Dad'll have to fight her for them.'

'He'll have to fight you for the microphone when the speeches start. I've already heard Ellie promising you'll give a talk about how you found the Cat Tomb.'

'Liar!'

'OK, her exact words were, "Amy would rather chew

off her right arm than speak in public." So your dad's going to entertain everyone instead.'

She sighed her relief.

He squeezed her hand again. 'Happy?'

'Um. Very. Just . . . Nothing!'

Nothing that mattered. She reached up and touched the necklace nestling at her throat – a present from Jason. It was a tiny wedjat eye. Symbol of healing and wholeness.

A guest group of schoolchildren came tumbling out of the rain and up the steps to the exhibition area. They piled their dripping coats on to clanging hangers, dutifully ignored their teacher's instructions, then fanned out around the museum to gawp at the displays. Most went straight to the mummy – a crabby-looking old bloke who'd been in the museum's stores since the year Queen Victoria first wore her crown. Some pupils pressed up against glass cases showing canopic jars, mercifully empty of pickled entrails. A select few took their phones out to photograph the rare mask of Anubis, god of embalming.

One eight-year-old girl with dreamy eyes found herself face to face with a small turquoise figurine. Fascinated, she read the information card:

**A magical *shabti* servant from Thebes, late 19th Dynasty, belonging to a young noble boy called Nakht.**
**(On loan from Cairo Museum. See also exhibits 20–29.)**

Nakht.

Funny name.

She copied it down in her jotter, so she wouldn't forget it.

Rain lashed the museum windows. Outside, on a wide sill, a tawny tom cat sat tall, watching the girl and the shabti.

One golden, glittering eye slowly but surely closed.

The cat winked.

# End Note

I very much enjoyed writing *The Glittering Eye*, but I have to admit it felt a little bit like cheating at times, because Egyptian history is so colourful and fascinating I hardly needed to make anything up. Paintings and stories give a vivid impression of the Egyptian afterlife, and astonishing discoveries are still being made in the Valley of the Kings.

Egypt is a wonderful country to visit. I don't think I closed my eyes the whole time I was there, particularly as our hot air balloon rose above the desert. Closer to home there are many museums with Egyptian artefacts on display or tucked away in their stores. I'd like to thank all the museums in Yorkshire that let me get *hands-on* with their objects (including a mummified frog!). I'm also very grateful to Dr Joann Fletcher and Dr Stephen Buckley for telling me about a tomb painting of a golden-eyed cat, along with many other more gruesome facts about life and death in ancient times. Of course, *The Glittering Eye* is a work of fiction, so plenty of imagination has been woven into the truth. I just wish my own clay shabti really was a magical servant, ready to answer, 'Here I am!'

## THE DIARY OF PELLY D

For Pelly D, her life stretches ahead, filled with glorious possibilities. But young building worker, Toni V, has just found her diary. Buried in a water can. In the rubble of a construction site. And with it, there's a note:

DIG, DIG EVERYWHERE.

It's against all the rules – he should just hand it in to the Supervisor – but Toni V is curious and he begins to read . . .

Buried beneath the sassy voice of a girl he's never met, he begins to sense another more sinister truth unfolding.

## CHERRY HEAVEN

i remember the last birthday i ever had was when
i got shot instead of presents where i come from
remembering's Against the Rules you only find out
what the rules are when you break them

i remember me

i'm Luka

### DON'T ANY OF YOU GET IN MY WAY

Kat and Tanka are looking for a bright new future
far from the bullet holes and bomb craters of the
war in the cities that tore their parents away.

A fresh start on the New Frontier.
A beautiful new home – Cherry Heaven.
Peace. Happiness.
No shadows.
But softly, secretly, shadows are creeping towards
them . . .